I'm fin
Don't worry about me.

She settled for "Let me do this my way. Please."

Rose grinned, her sweet face lighting up with humor. "You know that's not going to happen."

And then Mercedes, as she often did, Doris thought, broke through all her barriers and said the one thing guaranteed to force her to do something she did not want to do.

"We miss you," she said. "*I* miss you. You and Rose saved my life too many times, babysitting Julie, loaning me money, loving me when I believed no one else did. Or could. Please, Doris, let us help you."

"We can't get through the summer without you," Rose added. "Every day we don't see you is hard. We need to know you're all right."

"Sisters?" Mercedes said, holding out her hands to the two of them.

Rose grabbed first Mercedes, then Doris, her grip strong and sure.

"Sisters," she asserted. "Always."

Kate Austin

Kate Austin has worked as a legal assistant, a commercial fisher, a brewery manager, a teacher, a technical writer and a herring popper, while managing to read an average of a book a day. Go ahead—ask her anything. If she doesn't know the answer she'll make it up, because she's been reading and writing fiction for as long as she can remember.

She blames her mother and her two grandmothers for her reading and writing obsession—all of them were avid readers and they passed the books and the obsession on to her. She lives in Vancouver, Canada, where she can walk on the beach whenever necessary, even in the rain.

She'd be delighted to hear from readers through her Web site, www.kateaustin.ca.

KATE AUSTIN

THE GOSSIP QUEENS

isbn-13:978-0-373-88117-8
isbn-10: 0-373-88117-7

This edition published by arrangement with Harlequin Books S.A.

TheNextNovel.com

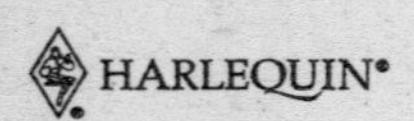

PRINTED IN U.S.A.

From the Author

Dear Reader,

The minute I finished writing *The Sunshine Coast News* I realized that Rose, Doris and Mercedes were still stuck in my head, clamouring to tell *their* stories. They had so much to say and insisted on saying it so loudly that I had to turn off the sound on my computer. This book—thanks to the three of them—was a lot of fun to write.

One of the things I thought about a lot when I was writing this book was how fortunate I am to have such good friends. I drew a great deal on the relationships I have with my friends for the interaction between Rose, Mercedes and Doris—the warmth, the comfortable nature of their conversations, their acceptance of foibles and eccentricities, and maybe most of all, the unquestioning support they give each other. The gossip queens take the time to celebrate and nurture their friendship and I hope that, from them, I've learned to do that as well.

I'd love to hear from you through my Web site—www.kateaustin.ca.

Kate Austin

For Heather—

with thanks for accepting my eccentricities.

CHAPTER 1

The most beautiful woman in the world was getting married and I wasn't at all happy about it.

Oh, sure, it seemed to be a good thing; Julie wouldn't be moping around anymore. And the groom, the police sergeant of our town, would be more focused on his job. Or would he? At least I hoped he would be.

But, after years of the two of them suffering from twin cases of unrequited love, the minute they got together, I felt the temperature rise. Not just *my* temperature, but the ambient temperature of the Sunshine Coast. I didn't want to think about how hot their relationship had to be to cause the mercury to rise all over the peninsula, but I couldn't help it. I'd been worrying about Julie's love life for so long I'd forgotten about having one myself. And the heat reminded me of just what I was missing.

I stood on the dock outside the Sand Dollar Motel and sweated in the bright summer sun. This rare moment of peace was an indulgence I didn't often allow myself once the summer—and all its joys and aggravations and hysteria—came to Gibsons.

The summer wasn't a time for self-reflection, that's for damn sure. So I went back up the hill to the motel and got to work.

Mondays were always the worst. The weekenders often waited until the last possible minute to get on the road—which meant a flock of screaming children and frantic parents crowded into my office at six in the morning, before I'd had time for coffee. They needed to be on the road by six-thirty to make the seven o'clock ferry, and with ten rooms and what felt like a thousand racing visitors, panic reigned for that first hour of the week. And continued right through until after Labor Day.

The good news was that, like every Monday, by the time the sun burned off the slight chill of the night, everyone was gone and I got ready to settle myself in to do it all over again. But not quite yet.

The thought of dealing with ten rooms' worth of sand and salt, the filthy towels and smelly, crumpled bedding made me want to vomit. I couldn't even bear to think about the bathrooms. Combine that with the fact that Julie, my only child, was getting married in September and I desperately needed a break.

I muttered as I hurried along the sidewalk in front of the rooms, checking the doors, locking those left standing open by the visitors in the stampede to get back to their *real* lives.

"I can't stay away long," I said, pulling doors closed without daring to take a peek at the chaos within, "but I need to get out of here."

I ripped off my official Sand Dollar Motel uniform—a golf shirt emblazoned with a starfish (a sand dollar just didn't have the oomph for a shirt)—replaced it with a lime-green T-shirt, pulled on matching sneakers and hurried down the hill to the Way-Inn to find coffee, a plate full of hash browns, and Rose.

I figured Rose and Doris had saved my life at least once. When Julie's dad absconded with the family fortune before Julie was born, Rose and Doris propped me up, babysat once Julie arrived and helped me buy a living and regain my sanity. I own the Sand Dollar free and clear now, but I always thought of my two friends as silent partners. Rose, Doris and me, Mercedes Jones—the three of us owned the Sand Dollar. But they weren't just partners in business, they were my partners in life.

I tried not to think about how much I missed Doris. Almost every morning—not in the summer, of course, but every other morning of the year—I'd meet Doris and

Rose at the Way-Inn. It wasn't always at the same time, but we'd been doing it for so long it was as if we could divine each other's schedule and Doris and I often ended up pulling our cars into the parking lot at the same time.

We'd sit in our booth in the back and Sam would wait on us. I grinned when I thought of poor Sam leaving his kitchen with a tray of coffee and hash browns.

Rose was the waitress, the hostess, the glue that kept the Way-Inn going. Sam was, without a single doubt, the best cook on the peninsula, but Rose… Rose was a miracle.

Just a few minutes with her, I knew, would rid me of the antsy feeling I'd been carrying around for days. Oh, it wouldn't get rid of it forever, maybe not even for the rest of the day, but it would damp it down considerably for a few hours.

Part of that feeling was Julie's wedding. That was the obvious part.

Part of it was Doris's ongoing absence. I missed her and I was pretty sure it'd be a while before I'd see much of her. Baby Emily wasn't the problem—we'd all spent hours with our own little ones at the Way-Inn and the beach—but Tonika's injuries were far worse than they'd first expected.

Poor Doris. She'd been looking forward to her first grandchild, not to playing mother to the baby and nurse to her daughter. Sixty-eight was too old for that kind of work. But Doris would never admit that.

I tapped my right temple, then spoke the reminder out loud.

"Talk to Rose. Maybe we can help with Tonika. Or the baby."

I'd been using the temple tap and verbalization for six months, ever since Rose sent me the link to the memory Web site. It seemed to help.

I pulled into the Way-Inn parking lot and smiled. Monday mornings were either frantic or dead slow and stop. Today was a dead-slow-and-stop Monday. One other car sat parked haphazardly in the lot. I didn't recognize it, so assumed it was someone from away.

The front door was propped open so the bell didn't announce my presence as I hurried through it. I missed the bell, too.

"God, Mercedes Jones," I whispered as I scanned the restaurant, "you are a frigging pathetic woman. First Doris, then Julie, now the bell? What is wrong with you?"

And then Rose smiled and raised her hand from behind the counter, wiggling her fingers and nodding her head toward the young man sipping coffee at the table in the window.

"Five minutes," she mouthed. "He has to catch the next ferry."

I settled into the booth at the back and watched the young man. There was something familiar about him, something I couldn't quite decipher. I didn't know him, I knew that much.

Or at least if I did know him, he was now out of context.

Waiter?

Teller?

Ferry man?

Delivery guy?

I closed my eyes and pictured him in each of the appropriate uniforms.

Nope, times four.

Maybe Rose would know. She never seemed to forget a face and she saw far more people than me. A summer after Rose had first seen her, a woman could walk into the Way-Inn and Rose might say, "How's your mother? Did she finally have her hip operation?" And this to a woman she'd seen once.

But there was something about this young man. Actor? Maybe that was it. *There's something about the way he moves*, I thought. *Something about the way his hands bring the coffee cup to his lips*.

Did it matter that I couldn't figure out who he was? On top of everything? It seemed to, because I couldn't take my eyes off him. I tried to remember to blink so he wouldn't feel my stare but my eyes began to sting, drying from the air.

I watched as he finished his coffee, smiled at Rose when he gestured for his bill, stood up and waited at the cash register while Rose giggled in the kitchen with Sam. I watched him pull a wallet from his pocket and hand money to Rose.

I saw him smile at Rose, a grin almost unbearably sweet, and I blinked away my tears so I could watch him walk out the door.

Whoever he was, it would probably come to me in the middle of the night. Or not.

I remembered no one—or very few people—and I envied Rose her ability, her joy in every story she heard, each smile she received. And today, more than anything else, I envied her Sam.

Short, yes. Definitely round. Never going to be a mover or a shaker (except on the dance floor), never going to set the world on fire. But he could cook like an angel and his love for Rose—and hers for him—shone like the April sun once morning's fog had burned off.

I pinched my thigh. "God, woman." I spoke to the old-fashioned salt and pepper shakers on the table. "What is wrong with you this morning?"

"Nothing that I can see." Rose laughed, sitting down with a tray of coffee and hash browns. "And you look fine to me. A little tired, but it's Monday."

"It's not Monday."

"It is so. Look." Rose grinned around at the empty room. "Of course it's Monday."

I groaned.

"Okay, okay, it's Monday. But *it's* not Monday, you see?"

Rose pushed the plate of hash browns closer to me.

"Ah, *it's* not Monday, I get it. Well, eat your hash browns first and then we'll talk about Julie. And Doris. And your pathetic—dare I say, completely nonexistent—sex life."

I mumbled through the hash browns, "I don't want to talk about it."

"Your sex life, you mean?"

I nodded.

"Okay. We'll talk about Julie. And Doris. But seeing as Julie's marrying one of the sexiest men on the peninsula and Doris is babysitting her granddaughter—who arrived because of an act of sex—sex is going to get in this conversation one way or the other."

I laughed and ate my hash browns. No eggs, no bacon, no toast. The three of us always ate hash browns when we were together for breakfast. Sometimes for lunch, too. We lived by that motto: Eat dessert first, although we'd amended it to read: Skip the protein, eat the hash browns.

"Do you know that man?" I nodded toward the coffee cup still sitting on the table near the window.

"I do now." Rose sipped her coffee and glanced at the window, a pensive look on her face. "But I feel like I should have known him even before today."

"I think he might be an actor," I said. "There's something familiar about him."

"That must be it. Because I could swear I've heard his voice before. Maybe he's on the radio."

I nodded. Rose didn't have time to watch TV. She probably hadn't seen a show the whole way through for twenty years. But Sam played the radio full-time in the kitchen, switching from station to station through the day. At night, he listened to the blues station out of Washington state.

That's what I always remembered about nights at

the Way-Inn—Johnny Cash or Elvis on the jukebox, with a blues chaser in between songs.

"Are you okay, honey?"

The worry on Rose's face almost broke me, but I raised my face to the ceiling and the incipient tears disappeared.

"I'm fine. Really. I'm just worried about Julie. And Doris. I miss her."

"I do, too. But I don't know what to do about it. That infection Tonika got just about killed her. And now her leg's taking forever to heal."

"I feel like we should be doing something."

I *knew* we should be doing something, but like Rose, I had no idea of what that something might be. And half an hour and two cups of coffee later, we still didn't.

"I have to get back to work. A dozen bikers are going to be here this afternoon and I haven't cleaned a single room."

Rose smiled. "Do you need a hand? It's pretty quiet here this morning."

"You can't leave Sam alone in the summer. It'd kill him if a tour bus pulled up and you weren't here."

"Okay, but don't say I didn't offer." Rose patted my hand. "We'll figure something out."

Maybe *we* wouldn't, but *I* was going to. Things couldn't go on as they were. I couldn't stand it much longer. The summer was only just beginning; I hadn't seen Doris in weeks and cut-short, unsatisfactory phone calls were no substitute; the wedding was ten weeks away; and, worst of all, I'd lost it.

I felt like I was spinning in circles, getting dizzier and dizzier, and I couldn't figure out how to stop it.

I'd lost my equilibrium, my power, my center. Lost it all.

CHAPTER 2

Rose watched Mercedes scurry out to her car and worried. She worried about Mercedes and she worried about Doris. She just wasn't sure which worry to deal with first.

So, as she'd done for most of her life, she turned to Sam. The kitchen sang around him, the dishwasher's low hum a counterpoint to the tinkle of glass through the washer. Burnside played gently on the boombox in the window, his ragged, mournful voice singing the blues Sam loved beyond— *Well*, Rose thought, *beyond everything except me*.

She knew neither Mercedes nor Doris really understood what went on between her and Sam. Oh, they'd loved men—at least she thought they'd loved the fathers of their children—but what Rose had with Sam? That was a miracle.

She knew people looked at the two of them and

wondered. She wasn't, by any stretch of anybody's imagination, a cover girl, but Rose had always been aware of her beauty, of men's attraction to her.

Most of that, she giggled as she looked down, could be laid at the door of her breasts. She ran her fingers down the sides of them. Men saw them first, often missing the humor and intelligence, the sweet, caring face that went along with the heft of them. At least that's what Sam always told her, and she chose to believe him.

Because he had looked right into her eyes almost thirty years ago and had never looked away.

Rose walked through the singing kitchen and right up to her man. She snuggled up to his back while he stood at the window, reached her arms as far as they would go around his more than ample belly—she often thought he grew it to match her breasts—and rested her head against his shoulders.

His voice rumbled through his back and right into her chest.

"You okay, love?"

"Hmm," she said, her lips tight against his T-shirt, "I am now."

He turned to take her into his arms and the inevitable sparks flew. Nothing could stop that zing of lust, not the strain of running a restaurant, the loss of their youthful, hungry bodies, the onset of menopause. They looked into one another's eyes and the fire bloomed.

"Later?" he asked.

"Not now?"

"Uh-uh. There's a bus pulling into the lot."

Rose didn't question him, even through the noise of the kitchen. Sam heard everything. He might not talk much, but he knew everything the gossip queens did.

He'd been the one to name them.

It had been pouring down rain that night. Rose had just shut the door on their first week running the Way-Inn and had collapsed, far past exhaustion, into the booth at the back with Doris, Mercedes, Tonika and Julie, the babies sleeping at the wall end of the benches.

"What's Brad Miller up to?" Doris asked. "I swear that girl's young enough to be his daughter."

"Actually, she *is* his daughter." Rose's head drooped on her neck and Doris reached over to massage it before she had a chance to say another word. "They dropped in for coffee this morning and I met her then."

"Yeah," Mercedes added. "Her mother just ran off to India with her yoga instructor and Beth wanted to meet her father."

"She looked him up at the library," Rose added.

That topic satisfactorily concluded, they moved on to another, more interesting, but much less easily dealt with subject.

"What about Ricky?"

"I ran into the sergeant," Doris said. "I mentioned the night wandering and he said he'd keep an eye out."

"His mama's getting too old to watch him now." Mercedes shook her head. "And Sergeant Yakimovich's not going to be enough. One policeman for the whole peninsula cannot worry about one boy in a man's body."

"I know." Doris got her faraway look, the one both Rose and Mercedes knew never to ignore. "I think we should start looking for a place they can both go, somewhere they will be looked after."

"What about Linda's?" Rose asked.

Doris's face lit up. "Yes, that might work."

"Linda needs the money and she'll feel a whole lot safer with Ricky out there." Mercedes took one more sip of cold coffee and stood up. "I've gotta go, but I'll call Linda in the morning. Doris, you talk to Mama. Rose, you call Jim at the real estate office. He can give you some idea of whether it'll make more sense for Ricky and Mama to rent out or sell the house."

Rose and Doris nodded. Another transaction

resolved in the way each of their transactions always was—any one of the three of them might bring a topic up, although it was usually Rose who saw the need before anyone else, Doris who mostly thought of a general solution, Rose chimed in with the specifics, and Mercedes ordered the logistics.

Sam appeared, as he often did, out of nowhere to help get the babies to the cars.

"Good night, gossip queens," he said, arm around Rose in the cool night air. "You did good work tonight."

And the title had stuck through the years, spreading right across the Sunshine Coast. Even newbies, people with no idea of how far-reaching the knowledge—and the power—of the gossip queens had become, had heard of them.

Rose and Sam saw it as a boost to their business. Some mornings almost half of the people in the Way-Inn were there to see or consult the gossip queens. But that was true only after Labor Day. During the summer, the residents of the Sunshine Coast were far too busy to worry about their own lives and the gossip queens abandoned their regular hours.

Rose laughed out loud at the foolishness of that thought. The three of them sat in the booth at the back, drank cups and cups and cups of black coffee for

Mercedes, Red Rose tea with milk and two sugars for Rose, and jasmine tea for Doris.

Those three pots and their matching cups were never used by anyone else. They sat on a special tray in Sam's kitchen and waited throughout the summer for their usefulness to begin again. Rose sometimes thought that was true of the gossip queens as well—waiting for their real lives to begin again.

Rose hadn't used those pots this morning. It just didn't feel right without Doris.

Through the morning, hustling to feed and water not just one but three buses full of elderly tourists up for a day trip to the Sunshine Coast, Rose fretted. It wasn't something she did much of but it was pretty easy to recognize.

Rose was the kind of woman who slept well, even now when she had to get up at least twice a night to deal with her shrinking bladder. It was funny how everyone told you that they'd lost inches as they got older. Or that their hair was thinning or their memory wasn't what it used to be.

All those things were important, of course they were, but the difference they made to a person's day to day life wasn't even close to the difference a shrinking bladder made.

Rose was extremely good at hemming pants and skirts. She'd never once bought one of either that had fit. Being five foot nothing guaranteed she spent a lot of time with a needle and thread.

She simply lived with the age spots and thinning hair and fragility. She was careful with her hand cream and her comb and how she walked.

But the thing they should be telling you, the thing they didn't talk about, was the bladder. Rose could remember going downtown with her grandmother, their route carefully planned to pass a public (or at least publicly available) washroom every few blocks. She'd wondered at the time how Granny had known, but she didn't wonder any more.

Rose, and every woman she knew over a certain age, had an internal map that included, in addition to streets and sights of local interest, the location of every washroom they could use in an emergency. And those emergencies seemed to occur every couple of hours.

Coffee shops, hotels, gas stations, public parks. Even friends who seldom left home or who left their doors unlocked for just this purpose.

Rose herself preferred hotels. Whenever she traveled to the city, she made it a point to stop in and pee at her favorite hotel. The recent renovations had made that stop even more pleasurable.

Rose continued to fret about Doris. She was worried

about Mercedes but felt pretty confident that Mercedes would figure out a way to deal with her own problems.

The three of them had long ago taken on certain roles, exactly the way sisters did.

Mercedes was the strong one. Rose had only seen her don the goddess of justice mask on one occasion, and it had been enough to scare her to death. Rose never wanted to see that again, even though at the time it had been necessary.

But Mercedes looked after herself, had brought up Julie on her own, built herself a business. And she had sex, not relationships.

Rose sometimes thought of Mercedes as one of those Corinthian columns, standing alone in a field of crumbled stone. She never seemed to falter, to question her ability to get to where she wanted to be. This time, though, Rose suspected that Mercedes wasn't at all sure of where that was.

Rose was the insightful one, the conciliator. She saw what people buried, their pain and fear. She was the warm one.

Doris was the reserved one, and she was also the one who reassured. One of her favorite lines was, "Oh, you have definitely done the right thing." Despite that capability for reassurance—and it really worked, Doris meant it in a way that almost no one ever did—Rose had seldom seen any emotion cross her face.

Oh, Doris smiled with them, but when it came to her deeper feelings, those stayed hidden, buried deep beneath her beautiful oval face. She didn't even cry when her husband had died a few years back, not even when Tonika, her only child, was so badly hurt.

Doris had explained it to Rose and Mercedes once, a long time ago. Rose had never forgotten her words.

"I was trained as a very young child to conceal my emotions, to avoid outbursts of any kind. By the time I reached school, it had become second nature to me. I wasn't a very happy child, not unhappy either, but no one, not even my family, could have known one way or the other."

Doris took another small, silent sip of her jasmine tea.

"Later, years after reserve had become the only way for me to deal with the world, I realized that perhaps there was a good reason for this training, a reason why my family insisted on it. Japan is a small country with a large population. Outbursts of any kind would disturb many people. I began to think of our reserve as the Japanese equivalent of the British stiff upper lip."

Rose now wondered if she and Mercedes should have worked harder over the years to break through that shell. Because now, stuck at home with the baby and Tonika, Doris's reserve was turning into isolation.

Before she had a chance to contemplate the problem, the phone rang.

"It's for you," Sam yelled from the kitchen.

Rose took a quick glance around the room. Everyone looked happy enough. No empty cups needed filling, no dirty plates needed to be removed, no menus left on any tables. She grabbed the phone.

"We need to do something about Doris. We need to do it now." Mercedes spoke with complete authority.

"You're right. I can probably get away in an hour."

Mercedes had, once again, read Rose's mind before she'd even had time to formulate the thought.

"I'll pick you up," Mercedes said. "I could use a cup of coffee I don't have to make myself."

"You can't call that sludge you make coffee. It's more like..." Rose giggled. "Pond scum. It looks and tastes like pond scum."

Mercedes hung up without responding.

"Sam," Rose called through to the kitchen, "I have to go out for a couple of hours this afternoon."

"Of course," he said.

Rose wouldn't have been surprised if he'd added the words, "you need to see Doris."

Rose often wondered whether her thoughts were louder than other people's, whether her mind somehow projected exactly what she was thinking into a bubble that hung above her head like the ones comic-strip characters used. Because both Mercedes and Sam, and occasionally Doris, seemed to know not just the general direction of her thoughts, but the exact words she'd use to express them.

"Nancy'll be in in a couple of minutes and the bus tours are on their way out."

"Don't worry, angel face."

Sam had left his kitchen to come up beside her, his arms around her shoulders. "Doris needs you. We'll be okay here."

She shrugged.

"What's the worst that can happen? A few customers get scrambled eggs instead of roast beef, or they wait an extra five minutes for their refills. So what? It's not gonna change the world. Doris, though, helping Doris might change some lives."

Rose sighed and settled against Sam's chest. He was right. He was always right.

CHAPTER 3

Doris opened the door expecting... She did not know what she had expected but it certainly was not Rose and Mercedes.

They stood on the porch, peacefully ignoring the crying baby, the mess in the living room, the uncut lawn. They carefully avoided any comment on Doris's unkempt hair and stained clothes. They waited for her to speak the way they always had, encouraging smiles on their faces.

Doris burst into tears.

Rose stepped into the doorway and pressed a tissue into her hand. "Come on, honey, let's sit down."

Mercedes pushed past both of them. "I'll get the baby and tell Tonika we're here."

"This has never happened to me before." Doris sobbed, appalled at her loss of control. "Not even once."

Doris was certain she had never cried in public before. She could not remember shedding even a few ladylike tears in public. She had certainly never sobbed. The embarrassment made her sob harder.

"It is so stupid," she wept. "There is nothing to cry about. Worse things than this have happened to me. Far worse things."

Rose rubbed her back exactly the way Tonika rubbed little Emily's. Richard did it, too. Doris did not. It was not something she felt comfortable with.

Doris cried harder. She cried while Rose rubbed her back, while Mercedes made and delivered a pot of tea, and while Emily got fed and then, happy, the baby stopped crying.

"Good," announced Mercedes. "Two people crying is too much for me."

Rose laughed. "One person crying is too much for you. Remember...?"

And they did, their memories circling back to just a couple of weeks after Julie's birth.

Julie was a beautiful and quiet baby. She slept through the night, she ate like a teenage boy and she hardly ever cried.

That was a good thing, Doris had thought at the time, because whenever Julie cried, Mercedes fell to pieces. The odd thing was that Mercedes did not panic. Mercedes was, most of the time, the most natural and comfortable mother imaginable. Doris envied her that naturalness.

Mercedes understood almost everything instinctually and was completely relaxed about it.

Crying was the exception.

Mercedes would pick Julie up, change her, feed her, rock her for no more than three and a half minutes, and then hand her to Doris or Rose.

"Here," she would say, thrusting Julie into whoever's arms were closer. "I'm a terrible mother. She won't stop crying."

Both Rose and Doris knew that, even including Mercedes's drive to find one of them, the baby could not have been crying for more than fifteen minutes and probably not even that long.

But the whites of Mercedes's eyes would be showing when she arrived. Her normally rosy cheeks would be pale and she would almost immediately begin hyperventilating. The sound of Julie's crying scared Mercedes at some level so deep she could not access the fear. So she could not deal with it.

Years later, when Rose was studying phobias—not for any reason that Doris could discern, except entertainment—Rose had printed out and given Doris a list of phobias.

She had checked to see if there was a phobia about crying but had found instead peladophobia (bald people), geniophobia (chins), chorophobia (dancing) and metrophobia (poetry). Doris was never quite sure why she could find phobias about poetry and chins and not one about crying, but there it was. No crying phobia.

Still, Mercedes did have one. When Julie cried, Mercedes panicked.

Mercedes seemed perfectly fine right now, sitting in the big green Naugahyde recliner, her feet up, a cup of steaming green tea held between her steady hands, while Doris sobbed and Emily had only just stopped crying.

"It's okay. Really. It's going to be fine," Rose said.

Doris tried to nod but it hurt her head too much. She stopped. She tried to say, "Don't worry about me," but the words refused to leave her throat. She tried, "I'm fine." They too were stuck.

It is nothing.

It is just hormones.

I did not sleep last night.

I have the flu.

Not one of those phrases would leave her mouth. She thought them. She moved her lips. Nothing came out.

Doris wondered what it would be like, never speaking again. She would have to carry a pad and a pen with her wherever she went, use e-mail instead of the phone. She would have to point at menus and would forever be unable to order a special meal.

She would be thought of as weird old Mrs. Suzuki. She would be thought of as *dumb*—not *mute*, which was the correct term—and it would not be long before they would add *deaf* to that description. She would still be able to hear but *deaf and dumb* was a natural kind of progression, so people would start yelling at her.

"HI, MRS. SUZUKI. HOW ARE YOU THIS MORNING?"

And even though she would hand them a piece of paper that read, I'm not deaf, even though she would eventually have these pieces of paper printed up by the dozens, people would ignore the words and continue to shout.

Quite quickly after that, she hoped, she would die, never having spoken another word.

"No," she screamed.

That word came out loudly enough to make Mercedes spill her tea.

"No."

Doris tried it again. The tears had stopped, and the single word sounded perfectly clear in her ringing ears.

She tried again.

"My head hurts."

"Of course it does," Mercedes replied. "Crying does that to you."

"It does?"

"Hmm. I'll get you some water and an aspirin. Are they in the medicine cabinet in the bathroom?"

I don't need... Those words wouldn't leave her mouth. *I am okay*. Those stuck, too.

Doris might have been feeling like an idiot, but she was neither stupid nor slow. "Thank you," she said.

Mercedes was watching her, an interested look on her face. Doris was willing to bet that Mercedes had it figured out before Doris did.

Mercedes would have absolutely no trouble recognizing magic. Or a curse.

Doris had seen it happen, but it took her a long time to acknowledge its existence. Mercedes did not don her goddess of justice mask often, but when she did, Doris thought, it was magic. Somehow she transformed into a higher version of herself, a woman who saw right and did it. Not a superhero, exactly, more a...

Well, Doris was not sure exactly what Mercedes

became, but she was confident that whatever it was, it *was* magic.

And while she was thinking about it, Rose had a little magic of her own. Less obvious than Mercedes's perhaps, Rose's magic was directed inward rather than outward, an ability to see rather than to do.

Doris envied both of them their magic, although she felt more comfortable with the brand practiced by Mercedes. Doris was not at all sure she was capable of seeing into other people.

Rose's ability to understand the despair of others grew out of knowing herself. Doris refused to believe in that old saying, 'Know thyself,' but Rose knew herself right down to the blackest carbuncles on her soul. She brought them out into the open, as if exposing them to sunlight would diminish their power. And for Rose, it worked.

For Doris? The very idea scared her to death.

Her upbringing had sealed her up as tight as Emily's belly when she was full of milk, so tight the skin almost thrummed with contentment.

In Doris's case, there was no contentment, only a very small measure of acceptance.

"I am who I am," she said out loud, her throat more than capable of releasing *those* words.

"Yes, you are," Rose murmured.

Doris quickly shook her head. She knew almost exactly what Rose would say next, and she wanted to avoid any of it. No *Doris, you're a wonderful woman.* She was barely a human being, and certainly not wonderful. No *We love you.* She knew they did and she knew she did not deserve that love. More than anything, she wanted to avoid the unbearably sweet *Doris, everything will be okay.* Because it would not be.

"I am too old for this."

She swallowed her aspirin.

"I am going to go back to work and help Richard pay for a nanny and a nurse. I cannot do this."

The tears threatened again, but Doris suppressed them. *There,* she said to herself, *that's better. The real Doris Suzuki is back.*

"You don't need to do that," Mercedes commented. "You just need a little help."

Doris snorted. "What month is it?"

"It doesn't matter. We can work something out."

"Which would involve the two of you paying for someone to help me instead of me paying for someone to help Richard."

Doris, when she did argue, won by logic, never emotion. But she seldom won against her two friends because Rose never hesitated to play the emotion card.

"Don't you care how we feel?"

"Of course I do," she said and then tried to continue. She wanted to say, *But this is the most sensible solution*. The words crammed up so hard in her throat she gasped. Those seven words locked themselves right below her chin and refused to move.

Mercedes's interested look had become avid.

"Doris," she asked, "can't you talk?"

Doris shook her head, trying to ward off the inquisition which was sure to follow. She pointed to her throat, pantomiming a cold. She touched her head, rubbed her throat, flaunted her reddened nose and eyes.

Mercedes laughed.

"Nice try, babe. You don't have a cold." She held up her hand to stop Doris from denying her claim. "You don't have the flu or bronchitis or laryngitis. You don't have strep. You don't have whooping cough. You don't have some exotic tropical disease that causes your throat to close up once every five minutes. You don't..."

Rose stopped her, giving Doris a momentary feeling of respite.

"Enough," Rose said to Mercedes. "Stop before you get to some obscure genetic defect you read about in last week's *New Yorker*."

Doris's shoulders settled back down where they belonged. They had been up around her ears with stress.

"It's not her throat," Rose continued, "it's her emotions."

"You think?" Mercedes joked. "Of course it is. But we need to figure out what triggers it. Why some words and not others?"

Doris tried to ignore the implications of that statement. Somehow, in the last few weeks, everything that had made Doris Suzuki's almost seventy years' worth of reserved and comfortable life possible had been stripped away, leaving this naked and quivering mass of uncontrollable emotion.

But she did her best to avoid further exposure. She smiled and sipped her tea, her hands as steady and dainty as she could make them. She concentrated on form, raising the cup smoothly to her lips, taking the most delicate of sips from its edge.

The routine, learned so many decades earlier, soothed her. She thought she might be able to convince them now.

Mercedes and Rose waited her out, their much larger hands engulfing the small porcelain cups, their eyes patient on her face.

I'm fine, she wanted to say.

But now she knew the symptoms and realized, even before the words were formed, that she would be unable to speak them.

She wanted to say, *Don't worry about me*, but those, too, would be impossible.

She settled for, "Let me do this my way. Please."

Rose grinned, her sweet face lighting up with humor. "You know that's not going to happen."

And then Mercedes, as she often did, Doris thought, broke through all her barriers and said the one thing guaranteed to force her to do something she did not want to do.

"We miss you," she said. "*I* miss you. You and Rose saved my life too many times, babysitting Julie, loaning me money, loving me when I believed no one else did. Or could. Please, Doris, let us help you."

"We can't get through the summer without you," Rose added. "Every day we don't see you is hard. We need to know you're all right. We need to help you with Emily and Tonika."

"Sisters?" Mercedes said, holding out her hands to the two of them.

Rose grabbed first Mercedes, then Doris, her grip strong and sure.

"Sisters," she asserted. "Always."

Doris watched them from beneath her bangs. These two women, though she had never told them, never before admitted it even to herself, were more her sisters than her own family.

She nodded and reached for their hands.

When the three sets of hands formed the circle, the light in the room turned golden, the air smelled sweeter and the birds in the neglected garden burst into a chorus of song.

"Now what?" Mercedes asked, abdicating her logistical role to Rose. "What do we do now?"

CHAPTER 4

The plan fell into place without much input from Doris. All she could do was nod as Rose and I worked out a schedule.

I watched Doris, noting what made her mute. Finally, after an hour, I figured it out.

"Doris. Don't say anything, just listen. These are the rules.

"You can't lie—well, maybe you can lie about your age or whether you like bananas. We should try that and see. But you can't lie about your feelings.

"You can't speak at all if you're planning on saying you're fine when you're not. Can you write it, I wonder?"

For the next fifteen minutes my curiosity got the better of my love of lecturing. I experimented, with Doris's very unwilling help, with the limits of the mutism.

I'd been right about the lying. Doris had no trouble saying she was twelve or that she hated liver and onions when she really loved them. She had absolutely no trouble saying how much she hated my lime-green sneakers. *Maybe*, I thought, *that was because she really did hate them*.

Doris tried a pen and paper. Same result as when she tried to say she was fine when she wasn't, though a different cause. If Doris tried to write that she was fine, she wrote only gibberish.

The ambivalent feelings were the hardest to pin down. If Doris really wasn't sure about something, she could go either way. The curse or psychosomatic disease or whatever it was only kicked in when Doris *knew* how she felt and wanted to say something else.

So the schedule was set, despite Doris's best efforts to stop us. In the end, she gave it over because we knew when she was lying.

It was kind of a payback, because in all the years I'd spent with Doris, I seldom, if ever, knew how she felt about anything. Rose may have had a better sense of it, but my knowledge about people came from their faces, not some instinctual knowledge like Rose's.

Doris's face, even at sixty-eight, continued to fall into a perfectly serene expression, no lines of laughter beside her eyes or her mouth—although she laughed when she was with us, as soon as she realized she was doing it, her hand came up to cover her mouth and she stopped.

Now I knew that this perfection resulted from training, not disregard. Doris *really* did care, she'd just never learned to show it.

In that, she was the total opposite of me. I revealed everything, often when I shouldn't. And that, of course, was the exact reason I was avoiding my beautiful and beloved daughter. Julie probably wouldn't let me get away with it for long, but for now? For now I didn't know how I felt, I just knew it wasn't the way a happy mother of the bride should feel. So I stayed away.

But back to Doris and her problems, far more serious than mine. Maybe I could help solve those, because I was doing a terrible job solving my own. I would do the morning shift, while Rose would put in a couple of hours in the afternoon.

And twice a week Doris would allow Richard to take over so she could go to the Way-Inn for a couple of hours.

"There," I said, clapping my hands together, "that's done and it's perfect."

"I can hardly wait," Rose said. "I can hardly wait to get my hands on that baby."

Of all of us, I thought, *Rose is the most maternal.* That was the source of her magic, her ability to see deep into people's hearts. And of all of us, she was the one who most regretted her past.

I remembered when Rose had first told us about the baby. The three of us had been sitting on the beach watching Julie and Tonika play in the tidepools.

Rose had watched for a few minutes, then turned her back on the water.

"Rose?" I asked. "You okay?"

"I can't watch the girls today," she said. "I have to go back to work."

"The Way-Inn's closed," Doris commented, her voice carefully non-committal.

"It's too hard," Rose said. "They're so happy, so beautiful, and…"

"And what? You can tell us, honey. It'll be fine." I pulled Rose down to sit on the blanket beside me. "You can tell us anything."

I wanted to know everything. I was lonely, starved for conversation, something more than Julie's little-girl talk and the demands of my customers. This was my chance. I wasn't a patient woman by nature but today I rubbed Rose's arm and waited.

"My boy is ten today. I keep thinking I'll get over it but I never do."

"Where is he?" Doris asked, her lovely voice somber,

somehow stilling the air between us until it felt as if the three of us sat outside the world.

"I don't know. I was only fifteen and I couldn't look after him."

I glanced over at Doris, hoping she would have the right words, but Doris's eyes had turned inward. Another secret there, but it would have to wait.

"Sam?" I asked, never stopping my hand moving up and down, up and down Rose's arm.

"Oh, he knows, but the baby wasn't his. I thought I'd be okay," she said, "and I am, mostly. Just once in a while..." She raised her head and smiled. "Once in a while, watching Julie and Emily, I really miss him."

Doris, as she often did, asked the question I couldn't get up the nerve to utter.

"Why don't you and Sam have children?"

"We can't. I can't. Not anymore."

"Why not adopt?"

"Maybe," she answered. "We talk about it sometimes."

I thought back to that day now. Rose had come to terms with her loss, channelling all that warmth and love into Sam and her friends. Even her customers. Seeing her now, I was sure Rose had done the right thing. Maybe not for herself, but for everyone around her.

I couldn't imagine the world without Rose in it,

mothering everyone she met, from tiny kids to big burly loggers. She watched over single moms and their exes, seniors in the nursing home down the street, strangers who stopped in for coffee.

She noticed when the hermit needed a ride home, when one of her regulars was in such despair they simply needed to be patted on the shoulder and told, "It's going to be okay. I know you don't believe it now, but believe *me*. It will be okay. Just hang in there."

Hell, she even mothered me. And if it hadn't been the busiest month of the year, if Doris's problems hadn't taken priority, if we'd seen more of each other, she'd have sat me down long before now.

"Mercedes," she'd have said, "what's up with you? Something's bugging you."

"Nothing," I'd say, because unlike Doris, lying remained one of my choices. "I'm just busy."

"Yeah, right. It's Julie and Ron, isn't it?"

"Yes and no," I'd say, prevaricating. Or not. But because this was *my* imaginary conversation, I'd allow myself to acknowledge the fact that I was insanely, foolishly, totally jealous of my daughter and the passion she'd found with the love of her life.

I might tell Rose that I wanted what Julie had—oh, not Ron, though he was gorgeous, especially since he and Julie had found each other. Add the joy with which he now viewed the world to the sharply pressed and perfectly fitting uniform, the spit-shined boots and the just-slightly-tipped-back Stetson, and you had the image of a perfect man.

But not for me. He was out of bounds for all sorts of reasons, not even including that he was the love of my daughter's life. Too young, too light-hearted, too... Too inexperienced, I guessed, which was an odd thing to say about a man who'd been a cop for ten years, but there it was.

If I was ever to have another man in my life—and that seemed increasingly unlikely given that I lived in a community where the number of bachelors older than eighteen could be counted on one hand—he needed to have been tempered in the blast oven of life.

He needed to know what it was like to live through something you believed might kill you. He needed to be older, for one thing, but that still wasn't the crux of it.

I couldn't explain it, couldn't even really do anything more than feel the idea somewhere in the back of my mind. I had no idea how to bring it forward into the light of day so I abandoned it. I was having an imaginary conversation, so who cared?

And I'm not at all sure it would have helped. Even

Rose at her most motherly couldn't solve my problem—at least partly because I couldn't even articulate it. Not to myself and certainly not to anyone else.

So, for now, I'd get back to the Sand Dollar, rush through the cleaning, and see if I could stop feeling as if I was missing something crucial in my life.

I was fifty years old and I had a longing. Maybe even stronger than that. Maybe what I had was a craving.

I picked up the phone in room three, the dust cloth dangling from my hand, the vacuum standing guard at the door.

"Rose," I said when she answered the phone, "do you feel like you're missing something?"

"Like lunch? Yeah, all that running around today really put me off my schedule."

I dropped onto the rumpled, unmade bed, something I'd never consider under normal circumstances. I didn't even cringe remembering the middle-aged man and the too-young, obviously-not-his-wife companion who'd vacated it this morning.

"Not lunch, you idiot. I mean something much bigger than that. I don't know. Do you miss having children?"

I listened while she settled herself. I could almost see her perched on the stool at the front counter, one foot tucked up under her, right hand holding the old black

Bakelite receiver to her ear, the other playing with the frames of her glasses.

"I did for a while, but it's not a generic thing," she replied. "I miss not knowing how my baby is, but having children? Nah. I have a wonderful life."

I sighed.

"I thought I did, too, but I'm questioning it."

"It's Ron and Julie, isn't it?"

My imaginary conversation was coming true.

"Maybe. But if it is that, if it's that I feel like I'm losing my daughter, why do I think it's more than that? So much more."

Rose took a sip of the Diet Pepsi that sustained her through the day. Diet Pepsi, Red Rose tea and plenty of coffee.

"What do you want, Mercedes?" she finally asked. "More than anything."

"If I knew that, we wouldn't be having this stupid conversation. I'd be out getting it."

She chortled. "Yes, you would, Mercedes Jones, that's exactly what you'd be doing."

"Oh my God, Rose. I've lost my mind. I'm sitting on a filthy bed. I've gotta go. Now."

I flung down the phone, leaped to my feet and into the bathroom which, thank God, I'd already disinfected. I ran the water as hot as I could bear and then ran my hands under it, scrubbing until they turned red. I put on a pair of rubber gloves and ran back to my room.

I gingerly removed my clothes—not easy considering I was still wearing pink rubber gloves—intending to replace them with clean ones and get back to work. But I got stuck standing there in my bra and panties.

I looked, really looked, at the woman in the full-length mirror and I didn't at all like what I saw.

Oh, the body was fine. Pretty good shape for a fifty-year-old. Maybe a little overweight, but that weight was in all the right places. Men, if there were men to be found, might call me Rubenesque.

The hair, now that was truly embarrassing. Too long for a no-longer young woman, faded brown and totally without shape. I would have to do something about that.

I held out my hands, still bright red from the scrubbing I'd given them. Bitten-short nails, age spots and scrapes on most of my knuckles—the result of deep-cleaning ten rooms a day. Definitely not attractive.

I got dressed—shorts, sneakers, T-shirt—still watching the woman in the mirror. The clothes, so innocuous, looked like hell on me. Beige shorts hanging to my knees bleached all the color from my legs, added twenty pounds to my frame, and turned my relatively shapely legs into stumps.

The dark-green Sand Dollar Motel shirt—chosen for comfort and washability—turned my complexion sallow.

Time to update my wardrobe, that was for sure. September was coming. Not soon enough, but it was coming.

I checked the mirror again, ignoring everything from the neck down.

The face was the real problem. I looked at myself in the mirror and saw a lonely woman. Damn. I hadn't realized it was so obvious. It hadn't been to me—not until this morning.

"Mercedes Jones—" I nodded at the woman nodding back from the mirror "—you're not going to turn into a lonely, sad old woman. Not if I have anything to say about it."

CHAPTER 5

All this upheaval, Rose thought, was having an effect on her work. She'd spilled tomato soup on her blouse, a beer on a customer—thank goodness he was a regular and more than willing to forgive her—and tripped over a Seeing Eye dog.

She'd given a woman a tuna salad sandwich *with* mayo when she'd asked for it without and—even worse, she'd given Josie Harris a plate of pancakes. Josie's face had blanched and she'd jumped up from her seat and left the Way-Inn. She'd called later to apologize but Rose was the one at fault. Josie hated pancakes.

Rose considered herself the best waitress and hostess on the Sunshine Coast, maybe in the entire country. She never forgot an order, never spilled a drop, and remembered her customers' foibles for years.

"This isn't good," she said to Sam as they sat on the sofa at the end of a very long day.

She had her back against one arm, Sam had his against the other and their feet were tangled together in the middle.

The sweet smell of hot chocolate and Grand Marnier mingled with the homey scent of toast and butter. They'd been eating the toast every night for years but the Polar Bears were a new thing. Josie had told Rose about them and, even though it was the middle of summer, they'd tried them and they'd stuck.

"What isn't good?" Sam asked, lazily running his feet up her calves.

"I'm a mess."

"Why? Because you spilled something today? Because you weren't your usual perfect self?"

Sam shifted so he could put an arm around her shoulders and pull her closer.

"Rose, you're the most amazing woman I've ever met. You never panic, you can deal with a room full of hungry, cranky seniors without breaking a sweat, you watch over everyone. Give yourself a break. You're allowed to have an off day. Really."

Rose wanted to protest but Sam was right. Those things were all true but something had happened today. Something important.

"It's not just an off day, love. I feel as if I'm an egg

and my shell is starting to crack. What if all my meat falls out?"

Sam laughed.

"Great metaphor," he said, "but I can't imagine you cracking. Maybe you're tired or worried. Things will be fine in the morning."

He patted her on the shoulder, kissed her temple, and said, "Why don't you have a sleep-in tomorrow? I'll look after the early birds. That's probably all you need."

That was the problem right there. Everyone, including Rose herself, saw her as unshakeable but they were all wrong. Rose really could feel the crack. It was small and quite thin, but it was definitely there. Maybe more like a ceiling crack than an eggshell crack. Rose was waiting for it to spread and the ceiling to collapse on top of her.

Rose had no experience in dealing with this kind of thing. She missed her son, she occasionally worried about the hermit or her friends, but she'd never before felt this fragile, this worried about her own self.

All Rose's worrying, the little that she did—Rose was more a doer than a worrier—was about others. She couldn't remember the last time she'd worried about herself.

And Sam's response—that she needed extra sleep—

would be echoed by Mercedes and Doris. They were so accustomed to her confidence and sureness of purpose that they'd simply assume she was tired or coming down with some bug.

And Rose wanted that to be true.

So she took her temperature. Normal.

She checked the calendar to see when her next period was due. Not for two weeks.

She stood in front of the bathroom mirror, lights on full, and her face mere inches from her mirror image. She checked her eyes for jaundice. White, not yellow.

She closed her eyes and stood still, checking her equilibrium for inner ear problems. Not a wobble.

She held out her hands in front of her. No tremors.

She coughed and sniffed. No phlegm.

She checked her armpits for faulty lymph nodes. They were fine. No pain. No swelling.

She slowed her breath and listened to her heart beat. Thump-thump. Perfect.

She filled her lungs. No fluid. No raspiness.

She even did a breast exam. No lumps.

Rose was running out of potential problems, so she dug deep and checked herself from head to toe for:

athlete's foot
rapidly growing moles
acne
sore muscles
miscellaneous aches and pains

She had none of the above and she'd had her annual checkup just a month ago. Her doctor, old-fashioned in words as well as manner, had said, "You're as healthy as a horse," and Rose, as she always did, wondered why a horse? Why not a cow? Or a dog?

But after her self-examination she had to concur with Dr. Hayes—she *was* as healthy as a horse. Assuming, that is, that horses sometimes suddenly felt as if they were fracturing into tiny pieces.

Rose shook her head and went to bed. Even with this weird thing going on in her mind, she was too sensible not to take advantage of Sam's offer. Rose loved to sleep and she didn't often get to indulge in a sleep-in. She'd enjoy every minute of it.

And she did, despite the odd sensation each time she surfaced enough to be aware of the ceiling moving above her. Rose ignored it, rolling over to snuggle up to Sam. Once he had gone downstairs to work, she pulled the comforter over her head, counted backwards from a thousand, and fell back to sleep somewhere around five hundred, having lost count and started over again half a dozen times.

Rose was determined to ignore the fragility she felt. Somewhere in the night she remembered that she was on the verge of forty—her birthday would arrive in less than a month. The cause of the mess was clear.

She'd loved turning thirty, finally feeling like a grown-up—not an easy thing to do for a short, baby-faced blonde. But obviously, forty was different.

Biological clock? Rose hadn't thought to check that last night. She concentrated. No ticking.

"Good," she muttered in the shower. "That's the best thing," she gurgled, her mouth full of toothpaste.

"I'm going to call the adoption agency," she said to Sam when she walked into the kitchen.

Rose didn't know when she'd decided to call; it certainly hadn't been a conscious decision, but had appeared in her mouth when she saw Sam at the range.

"I think you should," he replied to her statement, his hands full of red peppers and mushrooms.

Rose rounded the counter so she could check his face to see what he really thought. He smiled at her.

"Really," he said. "I'm surprised it's taken you this long to think of it."

Rose's shoulders relaxed. "I've got the information upstairs. I'll get it on my way back from Doris's."

She reached over, brushed Sam's hair back into place and kissed him. It started out as a thank-you-you're-always-there-for-me kind of kiss but it ended up as something quite different. The kitchen smelled of breakfast, the doorbell chimed, the coffee perked, while Rose and Sam sizzled right along with the bacon.

She finally broke away, her breath ragged. Sam's eyes had glazed over, the effect of the kiss on him visible in more ways than one.

He winked. "Remember where we were," he said and turned back to the grill.

Rose patted his butt and hurried out to the front. Nine o'clock and the hordes were arriving.

Rose's decision to contact the adoption agency seemed to have a calming effect. Plus, she was so busy she didn't have time to breathe, let alone worry about it. She raced from work to Doris's and back to work, enjoyed the occasional coffee with Mercedes and ignored the times when the cracks become too obvious to ignore.

She was convinced—or maybe she just wanted to be convinced—that once her birthday was over, once she'd talked to the adoption agency, she'd return to her regular self, the self who spent her concern on others, not herself.

She occasionally wondered if that was wishful thinking, mostly in the middle of the night when the ceiling crawled above her and she was starting over again at a thousand for what felt like the tenth time.

But she carried on. For the first time she understood what people meant when they said, 'Another day, another dollar,' or 'Just keep on keeping on.' She saw in her mirror the expression they wore when they spoke those phrases and she recognized it because she looked like them.

Their eyes were downcast, their lips still even if they were attempting a smile, as if they spoke the words from their chests rather than their throats. The worry lines between their brows always became pronounced, even if they seemed to be joking.

Rose had always jumped out of bed, eager to face the world. She loved her job, her husband, her friends. She loved her life. She knew that before this past few weeks she'd never seen that particular expression on her face.

She needed to talk to Doris and Mercedes. And more than just in passing.

It wasn't easy but she called Richard, arranged for Julie Jones to babysit Tonika and Emily, arranged for

Josie Harris to sit in at the Sand Dollar for an afternoon, arranged for extra help at the Way-Inn for the afternoon and evening and asked Sam to prepare a picnic.

She picked up the basket, the ice chest containing wine and beer and sodas, three lounge chairs, and then headed for the Sand Dollar.

She got Mercedes—whose face lost a bit of its sparkle when she saw Rose—then Doris—whose look of relief at being out of the house was the strongest emotion Rose had ever seen on her face.

She'd picked the most deserted beach she could think of. She'd called the woman who owned the summer house with private access and came up only on weekends, and the woman had willingly agreed. She was a huge fan of Sam's hash browns and she spent most of her weekends at the Way-Inn.

"Go ahead," she'd said. "Use it anytime. Here's the code for the gate."

"Thanks," Rose had replied. "We just need to get away for a bit."

"Yeah," the woman said. "I never think about that because I view the Sunshine Coast as a permanent getaway, but maybe it's not the same if you live there?"

"After Labor Day," Rose laughed. "Then it's a getaway."

It was the quietest and one of the prettiest stretches of beach on the peninsula. The sky shone as blue as possible and sparked diamonds off the equally blue water. A slight breeze brought with it the tang of salt and helped maintain the temperature at the perfect level.

Rose hated to spoil the moment, but she couldn't wait. She'd been practicing her speech, preparing for her revelation, all day.

"Sorry, but this meeting is about me. I called it so I set the agenda."

Rose handed Mercedes a glass of wine and Doris a wine spritzer. She gulped half of her glass of wine.

"Rose, it's fine," Mercedes said. "We're just delighted to be here, in the sun, at the beach. Take your time."

Doris nodded and lay back in her lounge chair, her body swathed in white cotton from head to toe. Only her toes peeked out from beneath her skirt and her fingers from her long sleeves.

"It's a beautiful day." She raised her glass at Rose. "I thank you for arranging it."

With those words, Rose realized that her agenda—ever so carefully planned, ever so ridiculously detailed—was unnecessary.

They'd talk, they'd understand, she'd feel better.

"It is a beautiful day. I'm going to enjoy it."

CHAPTER 6

Mrs. Doris Suzuki—for that was how she always thought of herself—sat on the lounge chair although she didn't lounge. It was not in her nature. Her back was straight, her chin up, her shoulders back, her facial expression in its usual placid state.

Doris had worked long and hard to school her face and she'd accomplished what she had set out to do. No emotions appeared on her mask except those she allowed. She had never managed the same with wherever her feelings resided within her skin.

She imagined herself as an inside-out mime. Instead of revealing everything all on the surface, Doris revealed nothing on the surface, while inside that mime revealed so much. She had learned to conceal but she hadn't learned to turn off her feelings.

She remembered when she'd first met Rose and Mercedes. She'd been older than Mercedes and Rose was even younger than Mercedes. Yet she cleaved to them as if they were the older sisters she'd never had.

They knew things, understood things, were able to reveal and discuss things which Doris in her wildest dreams could not have spoken about.

She believed they spoke for her when Mercedes said, "Sometimes being a mother is too much for me. I'm not qualified. I'm scared to death that I'll damage Julie forever."

Or Rose when she said, "I love Sam, he's the best thing in my life, but sometimes," she glanced around as if to make sure no one but Doris and Mercedes could hear her, "I find myself standing behind him and I can imagine myself hitting him over the head with whatever I have in my hand—frying pan, curling iron, baseball bat—and running away."

Doris had wanted to nod, to say that she felt the same.

She had wanted to do more than reassure Mercedes and Rose but eventually she settled into that role and, over the years, she'd come to enjoy it, to see its value, but she had always wished she could show her emotions, especially to them.

Well, she had got her wish. And if she had ever laughed when she heard the words, "Be careful what you wish for," she was not laughing now.

Doris's control had all but disappeared. The same appeared to have happened to both Mercedes and Rose. Not much surprise in that; their lives had often synchronized themselves. Any women who spent a lot of time together saw the symptoms of that synchronicity.

She'd read a study about a group of cloistered nuns who, after a few years together, began menstruating on the same day each month. All twenty-seven of them, not including the nuns who were too old for it.

The gossip queens had never gone that far, but they had been close. Within a month of Doris's husband dying, so had Mercedes's father, and Sam had had a cancer scare.

Now all three of them were worried about their children.

Doris thought about her morning. The baby's soft cries had reached Doris through the monitor, turned up as high as it would go. She hated to admit it, but her hearing was no longer what it used to be.

In some ways, she thought, that was a good thing. When she bathed Tonika, she could not hear the harsh intake of her breath each time she moved her leg. Or Richard's soft sobs from the kitchen in the middle of the night.

Neither of them could bear to watch Tonika's pain.

She was the only one who seemed to be coping with it. She smiled and said, every day, "I'm better." And maybe she was, but you could not prove it to Doris. Or Richard.

Tonika's mother and her husband put on their cheerful smiles in company—with Tonika and with each other—but alone? Each of them was a mess.

Doris's strict Japanese upbringing had prepared her for this. If anyone thought the British had stiff upper lips, they'd never seen a traditional Japanese family. Even babies were trained to keep their emotions inside. Tonika had learned that from Doris.

Doris wanted something different for Emily and maybe that was part of her problem now.

She did not know how to teach her granddaughter that it was good to show your emotions. Except, Doris giggled inside, maybe she was achieving it by example.

Emily's skin was often damp, made so by Doris's tears. She would come away from Tonika's room, from helping her to the washroom or bathing or trying to make her take the painkillers prescribed by the doctor, and she would pick up Emily.

She would sit in the rocker—the one bought specifically for Tonika, almost a foot taller than Doris—a cushion behind her back so her feet would touch the floor, Emily in her arms. She would rock Emily, whispering her fears to the baby. Doris knew she should not do it.

What if she damaged Emily beyond repair? What if Emily grew up believing the world a dark and dangerous and sad place?

Doris could not stop. Once she had begun speaking out loud, even if only to Emily, it became impossible to dam the words in her throat. And because she could not speak to anyone else, she needed to speak to Emily.

And she cried every time, salt water dripping down onto Emily's fine black hair. It did not seem to be doing any harm.

Doris checked every inch of Emily's head each week. No bald spots, hair longer and thicker each time she measured it. She had no way of doing the same assessment of with the baby's psyche. All she could do was hope.

Hope that the endless litany of regret and worry and pain was not somehow soaking deep into Emily's susceptible brain with the tears and changing the way she would grow up to see the world.

Because both Rose and Mercedes said Emily was the happiest baby they'd ever met.

"Does she ever cry?" Rose asked during one of her afternoon visits.

"Of course she cries," Doris said with a snap. "Mostly in the middle of the night."

The expression of shocked disbelief on Rose's face told Doris just how far she had gone. But she neither backpedaled nor apologized, just let the crankiness lie on the table between them.

Maybe she *was* getting the hang of revealing her emotions, although it seemed to be only the bad ones.

Mercedes had fared better when she'd said basically the same thing.

"Emily's such a cuddly baby," she said one morning. "Julie, now Julie was as independent as a cat from the day she was born. Oh, I could pick her up and feed her, but anything else? It just pissed her off.

"I swear she was picking out what she wanted to wear before she said a single word."

Mercedes rocked Emily and grinned. "She's so sweet," she said, dropping a kiss on the baby's forehead. "Sure makes it easier to look after her."

Doris allowed herself a nod. No words yet, but a nod was good, wasn't it? It expressed the emotion she wanted to convey.

Mercedes handed the baby to Doris. "See you tomorrow. Maybe I'll stop at the Way-Inn on my way out."

She raised her voice.

"Tonika, you want something from the Way-Inn tomorrow?"

Doris heard the two of them conferring from the bedroom. She knew that Tonika would say, "No, Mercedes, please don't go to any trouble for me," because that was what she had taught her.

She hoped Mercedes would ignore the first response—as she had learned to do with Doris—and insist.

Doris considered the disease she had acquired.

She called it a disease—her inability to speak white lies about her emotions—because that was how it felt to her. She felt infected by a virus beyond her control.

It reminded her of people taken over by aliens, somehow losing the ability to direct their own actions and feelings, being relegated to a life they were forced to participate in but which was beyond their control.

Doris's disease felt like that. She had convinced it to accept a minimal head bob—sometimes almost indistinguishable from her constant slight tremor—instead of using words, but that head bob was only occasionally enough.

More and more as the days passed she found herself forced to speak. She had snapped at Rose. That alone was an indication of how far the disease had progressed.

No one, not Sam, not customers, not even Mercedes, snapped at Rose. It just did not happen.

One day she said to Mercedes, "I am almost seventy. I am not sure I can cope. What if Tonika...?"

"Tonika is going to be fine. So are you. Maybe you don't remember how stressful it is to care for a baby but I do."

Doris smiled, a genuine full-face smile that reached her eyes (she felt them lighten when it did) instead of her usual careful lifting of the corners of her mouth.

"Remember that day you ran up the path with Julie in your arms and dropped her on the steps?"

Mercedes grinned and placed her reddening face in her hands.

"You did not even ring the doorbell, just ran back down the street and phoned me from the corner to tell me she was there."

Mercedes groaned again. "I've never told Julie that story."

"At least I have not done that to Emily," Doris said. "At least I have not gone that far."

But Doris knew she had been close to something far worse. She had considered disappearing, just leaving Emily and Tonika and Richard to make it on their own. Because she believed they would be better off without her.

She had planned it during those sleepless nights when she listened for Emily and tried not to hear Tonika's pain-filled voice at the same time.

Doris had plenty of money, most of which she would leave for her family. She would go to the city, get a room in a boarding house under another name. She had seen enough television to know what to do. Pay cash for everything, stay below the radar. She would take the long way to the city, not the direct route.

And she had one thing going for her that the police procedurals never mentioned. No one—well, hardly anyone—noticed women of her age. It was as if they were invisible or so natural a part of the landscape—like dandelions or gravel on back lanes—that they passed right across people's sight without registering.

In the end, Doris stayed. She was unclear as to why she stayed, but she had her suspicions.

Being forced to speak had changed everything.

•

CHAPTER 7

I wasn't having my favorite summer. Busy with the Sand Dollar at the best of times, I'd added a couple of things to my schedule:

1. Two hours a day with Emily. I loved the time with her but it was two hours I could ill spare.
2. Somewhere between five and a hundred phone calls a day from Julie, ranging from "Should I wear white?" to "How many roses should I order?" to "It's okay to have the dogs at the ceremony, isn't it?"

My answers, after I'd soothed her panic, were "Of course," "Ten dozen," and "Yes, but make sure you bathe them first."

What did I know about weddings? I'd never had one.

Add Rose and Doris as well as Emily and Julie to my plate, and it was more than full; it was spilling all over the floor and making a helluva mess in the process.

Doris, my role model of quiet and reserved perfection, had lost it. Completely. I'd known her for twenty years and never seen a single tear on her face. Not even when her husband died. She was making up for all those unshed tears in one summer.

And Rose? Sweet, relaxed, happy Rose? She fidgeted. She fussed. She fretted. I hadn't quite figured out the reason, but I wasn't going to wait too much longer to ask.

Oh, yeah, and I forgot the other wedding. Julie's friend, Josie, was getting married as well, and her mother was off somewhere traveling so I fielded her questions, too.

The good thing about all this activity—well, two good things actually, were that I didn't have any trouble getting to sleep—I fell into bed and was out almost before my head hit the pillow—and my longing, brought on by Julie's romance, had settled to a dull roar.

It was still there. I noticed it most often in the early mornings in those few moments before I dragged myself out of bed to face another frantic day.

My body, relaxed and warm, would begin to heat

and, without any sensory input from me, the cravings would roll over me like waves. The first day this happened, I'd imagined—I was that age, after all—that I was suffering a hot flash, but I soon discovered that the heat was nothing so simple.

It was undirected lust, at least part of it was. Maybe the biggest part. But it included a desire to be held and a longing for another body, a male body.

Those mornings forced me to acknowledge how much I'd missed the feel and smell, the taste and touch of a man's body.

I'd had the lust before and dealt with it, but the longing was new and much, much harder to deal with.

Forget the fact that the only single men on the Sunshine Coast were either teenagers or geriatrics. Forget the fact that the community was so small that every single person in it would know within an hour if I, by some miracle, had a date. Forget the fact that I'd never really had a relationship with a man and I was fifty years old.

None of those things—okay, maybe the last—had anything to do with the stark, raving terror that accompanied the longing.

Longing was so much more than lust, more than fun, more than… More than I'd ever had or wanted with a man.

I tried to put it down to menopause but I knew I was lying to myself. Just as Julie had longed for Ron, just as Rose now longed for her son, I was longing for something I'd never had.

Watching Julie and Ron, the way they looked at each other, the way they couldn't seem to be more than three inches apart whenever they were in the same space, made me green with envy. And green wasn't my color.

My usually red-tinged cheeks actually turned the most unattractive shade of green you could imagine. I'd look at myself in the mirror and I'd see a woman who needed to stop envying her daughter's joy.

But as easy as it was for me to recognize the problem, I couldn't solve it.

I began walking on the beach in those early mornings, trying to shake off the longing, pulling on jeans and a T-shirt, not even bothering with shoes.

I'd be on the beach, my feet scoured by the cool wet sand, just as the sun rose behind me. It bounced light off the dark water, turning it into a kaleidoscope of color. Reds and pinks and oranges of every imaginable hue battled with blues and greens for supremacy.

I walked three miles up the beach, the sun gradually warming both me and the air around me, as far as the hermit's cottage, stopping just short of what I, what we all, thought of as his property line.

I sat on the rock farthest out on the natural spit, the water softly murmuring, the gulls waking and starting their "me, me, me" calls.

The water soothed me, making it possible to ignore—for just a few minutes—the exhaustion and to sublimate the longing to the beauty of the morning.

Two weeks into my routine and I felt better, stronger, less uncomfortable in my own skin. This morning, my new habit well established, I'd even managed to make and bring a thermos of coffee with me. The view, the sounds of water and gulls, the pungent scent of low tide together with the life-giving aroma of dark French roast, all conspired for a moment of perfect peace.

"Mercedes Jones?" a low, soft, husky voice—a voice as deep and dark as the French roast I was drinking—questioned from the shore.

The perfect peace shattered. Who in the hell had been walking around the Sunshine Coast with a voice so sexy it practically dropped me in my tracks?

I didn't want to turn around. I knew everyone, and not a single man on the peninsula looked the way that voice sounded. Once I turned, I knew I'd be disappointed by the reality. So I stayed, my face firmly turned out to sea, savoring the echo of that voice.

"Mercedes?"

Its power undiminished, I shivered on my rock and pulled my feet up under me.

"Go away," I whispered. "Please, before I have to turn around and ruin the fantasy I'm planning on living with all summer. Go away."

I knew he couldn't hear me but I hoped he'd get the hint from my body language.

"Mercedes Jones."

The soft voice turned to a roar and my fantasy crashed into the ocean to be pecked into nothingness by the gulls around me.

"Tell me I don't have to come out there and rescue you," the voice, once again its luscious self, sounded closer.

I picked up the cup I'd been cradling between my knees and kind of waved it in the air over my head. I hoped he'd take that as a sign of my sanity.

"Are you offering? I've brought my own cup."

I was still refusing to turn around but I could hear that even if I didn't move, the man, whoever he was, would soon be at my side and I'd have to see his face.

The disappointment colored my response.

"No, I'm not offering. Get your own damn coffee. And what are you doing wandering around the beach at this hour of the morning with an empty cup?"

"It wasn't empty when I started, of course."

He was right beside me. I childishly twisted away so I wouldn't have to see him.

"Idiot," I muttered.

"I know," he replied. "Who else would clamber out onto these unsafe rocks?"

"I was talking about me, not you."

"So was I."

The unjustness of that response pissed me off enough to turn my head toward the voice before I started to yell at him. A tall thin shadow stood silhouetted against the rising sun and my longing—totally without my consent—settled on its object.

A voice.

Because I still couldn't see him. What I saw was this: a tall, thin figure limned with an aura of blood-red and rosy pink. Wisps of hair, too long for fashion, blew around his face. One hand dangled a coffee cup.

"I'm not an idiot," I said to the shadow. "This is *my* beach. I know the tides. I know the rocks. I come here every morning *to be by myself.*"

The emphasis on those last words wasn't anywhere

near as strong as it would have been five minutes ago. Back then, I truly believed that my solitary morning hour on the beach was the only thing saving my sanity during this far-worse-than-usual summer. But now?

I wasn't stupid. It wasn't going to matter one bit who this man was—old, young, single, married, rich or poor, gay or straight—my undirected lust, my lifetime's worth of longing had attached itself.

I tugged at it to see if I could shift it, but the line attaching us was solid. I poured my still-steaming coffee on the line I saw faintly gleaming on the rocks between us. It sizzled and solidified, as if heat was its natural element.

"Damn," I whispered. "Now what?"

"Now you pour me a cup of coffee," that perfect voice said, "instead of wasting it on the rocks."

A hand and a cup appeared from over my shoulder. These I could see. The cup was the pebbled copper of the plates I'd bought at the summer craft fair from a couple who lived so far up the mountains we only saw them once a year—at the August long weekend.

"Nice cup," I said, wishing I'd bought them myself.

"Pour the coffee, Mercedes. My mouth is watering."

So was mine. The hand holding out the cup was colored deep brown. Not tourist brown but spend-all-year-in-the-outdoors brown. A fisherman, a builder, a…

"Mercedes?"

The cup wagged in front of me as if to say "I'm waiting." I poured the coffee.

"You'll have to drink it black."

"That's the only way," the voice said as the hand and cup disappeared back over my shoulder. "Thanks."

I sat there, the thermos once again cradled between my legs, and listened as the sound of the footsteps faded away on the rocks. I couldn't seem to turn around, couldn't lift my eyes from the water, couldn't convince myself to find out who owned that voice, those equally beautiful hands, and knew my name to boot.

Because sure as shootin', knowing wasn't going to do me any good.

There was no man on the Sunshine Coast, no *suitable* man on the Sunshine Coast. So what if my longing had fixed itself on this man? I could not put a voice and hands and the outline of a body in my dreams.

I didn't have to do anything about it.

Did I?

CHAPTER 8

The afternoon on the beach helped. Not a lot, Rose thought, but enough.

Because it felt so good to be on the beach with Doris and Mercedes, because the sun was shining and the beer was cold, Rose forgot why she'd called the meeting.

She forgot the fragility, the sleeplessness, the anxiety, the disconnectedness. She forgot calling the adoption agency. She forgot the cracked ceiling, the crushed meat of the egg, and the hot flushes. She forgot it all and concentrated on the sun and the sand and the sound of water.

That sound reminded her of when she'd first met Sam and the way she swore she heard his heart beat from across the room, the rhythm of it so much a part of her that it never left her, even when they were apart.

Rose had spent all of her life within earshot of the ocean. She'd seen it in every single mood and sometimes it scared her.

But today? Today was the kind of day Rose lived for. You had to concentrate to hear the water, a sound just slightly below comfortable hearing range, a murmur rather than a roar. Like a lover's voice in the night.

"I needed this," she said to Doris and Mercedes as they packed their gear back across the sand to the car.

"But we didn't talk about..." Doris shrugged. "What was it?"

Rose grinned.

"It doesn't matter. I'm fine now."

And she really thought she was. Almost.

Instead of three or four hours of sleep a night, she was up to five. She could cope with that; she'd done it all the way through her twenties.

Rose laughed when she thought of it. She remembered bragging about it as if sleeping less meant you were a better person than those lazy buggers who slept more. It had been the eighties, after all. Over-achieving—even in hours of sleep—was everything.

But she had to admit that five hours was no longer enough. Not even close.

She felt herself becoming lighter. Whatever connection she'd had to the earth, to her place on it, was weakening as she got less and less sleep. She had to be careful, she realized one day when she'd raced across the Way-Inn and almost hit the front door. She hadn't been able to stop herself, as if the momentum of her passage across the room had been too much and she'd begun to lose touch with the floor beneath.

Like an airplane taxiing across the runway and the wheels finally, slowly, inevitably leaving the ground. That's what happened to her.

She'd pictured herself spinning off the earth, out into orbit. She'd join all those defunct satellites and other space junk in slow, stately circles around the planet. Occasionally, she'd wave to the astonished men and women in the Space Station. She knew they'd never speak of her appearance in their windows. Too *X-Files*, too *Outer Limits*, too easy to get pulled from the program for insane behavior.

Rose slowed down. It was the only thing she could think of to avoid the disaster she'd imagined.

The weird thing was that no one noticed. Not even Rowena Dale, who noticed everything.

They would put their not-quite-so-hot coffee and cooling toast down to the rush of the summer. They'd say, "Rose is busy, that's why she's forgetful."

Sam wouldn't even notice. He believed everything Rose did—up to and including breaking cups or spilling beer on customers—was exactly as it should be. And while normally Rose loved it that Sam loved her without a single reservation, there were times when she wished he'd notice when things weren't going well.

Except, of course, he didn't have much experience with that. Because their life together had been pretty much perfect.

But there was the time she'd been so worried about the hermit, more worried than normal, she meant. He'd only been on the beach a couple of years at that point but she already understood his pain.

It was winter, much colder than usual. In fact, the weather guys were talking about snow, and while the kids—and a fair number of the adults, too—were looking forward to it, Rose worried about the hermit. Sure he had a stove in his hut, but still. Snow was a whole new ballgame.

She spent most of the next few days pacing the restaurant, back and forth from the kitchen to the windows, peering out through the steam to see if a single flake was falling.

Three days went by, the anticipated snow failed to appear and Sam didn't notice a thing, although Rose was certain she'd worn a path in the linoleum. In fact, if she remembered rightly, that had been the year they'd had to replace the flooring.

And now?

Sam patted her shoulder or her butt or her breast each time she passed through the kitchen, smiling his big gorgeous grin at her, but he just couldn't see that she was screwing up, big time.

Mercedes saw it, though. She saw it right away.

The day after Rose had pictured herself circling the earth, Mercedes dropped by on her way out to Doris's house.

"Tonika wants shepherd's pie and make sure you burn the top." She raised her voice so Sam could hear her in the kitchen. "Doris wants wonton soup with noodles and I want grilled cheese. Don't forget the fries. For all three of us."

She grinned at Rose who said, "You do know it's summer, don't you?"

"Yep. But grilled cheese is good all year round and what Tonika wants, Tonika gets."

"She is feeling better, isn't she? I thought yesterday..." Rose hesitated and then continued, "I thought the pain wasn't quite so bad."

"Me, too, honey."

Mercedes squeezed Rose's shoulder. "I really do think she's recovering."

"It's so slow."

"Nothing we can do about that," Mercedes said, leaning against the counter. "We just have to wait it out."

Rose sighed and turned to the coffeepot, banging her hip on the pass-through and knocking a dirty plate off and onto the floor, where it shattered.

"Rose?" Mercedes's voice sounded shrill. "You okay?"

"I'm fine."

Rose waved off the question but she knew Mercedes, as unlike Sam in this as it was possible to be, wouldn't let it go.

"I've broken more china and glasses in the last month than in my entire working life."

Rose stooped to pick up the big slabs of dirty white plate, her back to Mercedes at the counter. There, she'd admitted one of her symptoms. Now if she could only figure out the cause.

A soft arm came down around her shoulders.

"Sit down," Mercedes said, helping her up from the floor. "I'll pick that up."

"I can do it."

"Of course you can, but why should you? Have you ever heard me offer to do anything in a kitchen except pay for a meal?"

Rose laughed and the laughter, plus seeing Mercedes on her knees on the floor in front of her, released something in Rose's heart. She couldn't stop laughing, until the laughter turned to giggles, strong and unstoppable.

She felt her face turn red and her heart begin to pound. Tears poured down her face and still she couldn't stop. Her throat hurt and her cheeks cramped and still she laughed, still giggled.

"Something's wrong with me," she whispered through the laughter, knowing only Mercedes was close enough to hear the words. "It's serious," she continued. "Maybe I'm going crazy."

The look on Mercedes's face was enough to tip Rose over the edge from laughter into hysteria. The giggles welled up, bursting into the air around her until the entire room seemed full of them like champagne bubbles in a glass.

Rose backed away as Mercedes stood up. Rose was still laughing.

"Don't," Rose sputtered. "Don't. I'm okay," she told her while still giggling and unable to stop.

Mercedes pulled back the hand she'd obviously been readying for a slap and grabbed the water pitcher.

Rose held up her hands. "Don't. Don't. Don't."

She knew the words wouldn't stop Mercedes if she thought Rose needed it, so she tried holding her breath to stop the laughter. It didn't work. Maybe Mercedes knew what she was doing.

She did.

The dousing of cold water stopped the laughter in its tracks. Rose smiled through the water pouring down her face.

"Thanks. I needed that."

Mercedes nodded, her beautifully shaped eyebrows meeting right over her nose.

"You did."

Rose smiled again and nodded back. She felt the hysteria just beneath her skin waiting for her to lose control again. Now she knew it wouldn't take much—a sad story in the paper, one of her regulars having a bad day, an extraordinarily funny joke or a dead fly on the windowsill.

Rose slowed even further, slowing her emotions along with her body, working hard to get control of them as she had with her almost lighter-than-air body.

Mercedes had knelt on the floor, still watching her, pieces of plate in her hands. "Rose?"

Rose shrugged. "I don't know," she said. "I've wasted hours and hours and hours when I should have been sleeping trying to figure it out. All I got were these." She pointed to the bags under her eyes. "No answers."

"Not your son?" Mercedes murmured.

"Sam knows," Rose spoke in her regular voice. "No need to whisper."

A big voice boomed from the kitchen. "I know everything, Mercedes Jones, so don't strain yourself trying to hide it from me."

When she didn't respond, his head popped out of the pass-through. "What are you trying to hide from me?"

"She asked me about the baby," Rose said.

"Oh. Well, then, carry on." And he disappeared back into his natural environment.

"It's not the baby. I've done all I can. Written to the agency. If he starts looking for me they'll tell him where I am. And that I want to meet him."

"So, what?"

"Don't know. Not really. I just know the symptoms."

Mercedes stood up, and raised her voice. "Sam, we need some tea."

Sam yelled something that Rose didn't catch, then a few minutes later a tray appeared bearing a teapot, cream, sugar and two cups. Mercedes grabbed Rose's arm and tugged her back to their booth. She poured the tea and waited.

No one in the world was better at waiting than

Mercedes. She sat as still as a cat outside a mouse hole, her eyes bright and unblinking.

"I can't sleep. I worry. About Doris and Tonika. About Sam. About the Way-Inn. About you and Julie and Ron and the hermit. I even worry about getting old."

Mercedes sputtered at that.

"You're still a baby. Not even forty. If you wanted another child you could still adopt. Lots of women your age do."

"It's not that."

"I know. I'm just saying. Wait ten years before you worry abut getting old, okay?"

"Don't ask me how I feel," Rose finally got the nerve to say, "and then discount what I say. You all do it to me as if I can't be sad or unhappy or worried. Even Sam thinks I just need some sleep."

Mercedes blinked and reached across the table for Rose's hands.

"You're right. I'm sorry, that wasn't fair." She poured more tea and settled back into stare mode. "What else?"

"I never used to worry. I would do what was necessary but I didn't worry. I know it doesn't help but now I can't stop it."

"And?" Mercedes asked.

"And I have nothing to worry about. Doris has

something to worry about. Tonika has something to worry about. Julie has the wedding to worry about. You have Julie to worry about. Me? I have the perfect life. I have nothing to worry about."

"And?"

"And I feel like I'm losing it, like I'm cracking, literally cracking, like my skin will just split open and what's left of me will spill out. I'm out of control."

"Don't hit me for saying this, but maybe you need a vacation?"

"Nope. It's bigger than a vacation can solve."

"A therapist?"

"Where would I go? There's no one up here and I can't afford the time to go to the city."

"Okay."

Mercedes straightened up and her face seemed to take on an added power.

"Okay," she repeated. "You need to make it through the summer, right? Then, if you still need to, you can take the time for a therapist."

Rose considered it.

"Six weeks," she said. "I need to get through the next six weeks."

"No problem." Mercedes grinned. "I know just what to do."

CHAPTER 9

Doris began to believe that her loss of control was over, that she had—by sheer force of will—overcome whatever had overcome her.

She blamed Rose and Mercedes for the short, uncomfortable bump in her generally serene life. It *was* their fault. She had watched Mercedes's temperature rise as Julie and Ron's wedding got closer. She had watched Rose's usually calm and relaxed attitude turn frenetic.

Of course she caught whatever they were dealing with. The three of them had spent so much time together over the years that cross-contamination was inevitable.

But Mrs. Doris Suzuki knew she was capable of coping with anything. She would resolve this problem because she did not want to run away, she did not want to abandon her family and friends despite the fact that it was their fault she had ever needed to consider it.

Her mind and emotions seemed to have settled

down. She was once again able to ignore whatever went on beneath the surface and concentrate on the face she presented to the world.

Doris felt safe again.

That, of course, was a mistake.

She had seen enough movies, read enough books, to realize that one should never become complacent. The moment one makes a statement like "She felt safe again," the screenwriter would yell— "Drat, we need another tiger." Or earthquake. Or more pirates.

Doris knew this. She was unsure as to why she had so foolishly tempted fate in this way, but she had, and she was now required to suffer the consequences.

Emily reached the crawling stage on exactly the same day that Tonika's doctor told her it was time to begin physiotherapy.

The pain and potential disaster quotient increased exponentially while Doris's ability to cope did not. She had made it through Tonika's accident, through the premature birth, through the weeks in the hospital, the months at home. This, though, was too much for Doris.

The physiotherapist arrived bearing instruments of torture. Doris watched as she turned the living room— the biggest room in the house—into a combination gym and torture chamber.

All the soft, comfortable furniture was pushed back against the walls or moved to the garage, totally destroying the peaceful family space Tonika had worked so hard to create.

A massage table dominated the room. Various straps and ropes and pulleys hung from the table, from door handles and picture frames. Large purple and pink balls rolled across the—only now obvious to Doris—distinctly unlevel floor, their colors an affront to her eyes.

A small rolling table contained lotions and potions and unguents. The room, instead of smelling of incense and woodsmoke, now smelled like a combination of hospital and perfume counter.

The metal contraption next to the table was the worst. Everything else—except the straps, of course—might have been used in a high-end spa or salon. The metal frame was too obviously made for pain and Doris did not want to imagine what torture Tonika would endure once arrayed on it.

She did not have to imagine it. She not only had to witness the torture, she had to learn how to administer it as the physiotherapist came only twice a week.

"Mother," Tonika told her after the first consultation, "I need to do this every day to get better."

"I am not strong enough," Doris replied, not meaning physically, but hoping that was how Tonika would interpret her words.

"Yes, you are. And I want to be well enough to play with my baby before she goes to school."

Tonika had always been good at playing the guilt card and Doris very bad at resisting her. So she went back to school to learn new and ingenious ways of torturing her daughter.

She learned massage techniques that caused sweat to stand out on Tonika's face and her teeth to grind so Doris swore she could see them getting smaller every day. She learned to use the straps and pulleys to stretch muscles months out of use, muscles which quivered and popped as she did it.

Doris even learned to use the hated metal contraption. That was the worst of all. When she helped Tonika to stand within it, it was all Doris could do not to run screaming from the room.

She did not know how Tonika could bear the pain.

"I do it for Emily," Tonika said, over and over again through the tears, a mantra Doris believed she used to help her exist with the pain. "I do it for my daughter."

And so, too, did Doris.

"I wouldn't do it otherwise," she said to Mercedes

or Rose, who occasionally witnessed the torture sessions. "She makes me do it."

Her friends responded as they always did, with love and compassion, and in Mercedes's case, a good strong dose of common sense.

"If you don't do it, she'll try to do it herself. Not a good idea."

Rose added, "I think it's one of those things that gets better as it goes on. You just need to get through the first couple of weeks."

She rubbed Doris's back, her hands as soft and warm as Emily in the night. "You'll see an improvement soon. I promise."

Doris did not see how Rose could promise anything. But Doris tried to take her advice, one single day at a time.

She did know that she would not have made it through even one of these new, exhausting days without Mercedes and Rose. Not just because they helped her with Emily but because they gave her something other than Tonika to worry about when she collapsed into bed each night.

Because beneath Rose's love there was panic. And because beneath Mercedes's common sense there was... What? It gave her something to contemplate in those hours before dawn while she tried to steel herself for the day to come.

She pieced together clues from Mercedes's behavior, from her conversation, even from her clothes. And decided, one morning just as the sun hit her window, that Mercedes's lust—Doris had seen what bothered Mercedes long before she had done so herself—had settled on an object.

Doris understood that because once Mr. Suzuki had died, Doris herself had gone through a similar phase. Longing for a man's body in bed next to her. Doris was well past that now but she had no trouble recognizing it.

Contemplating who that object might be helped Doris as she spent two hours a day torturing her daughter.

She ran through the list of possibilities as she made Tonika moan, sometimes even cry in pain. She had started trying for a list of eligible men but as that was so short—almost nonexistent—she moved on to men in general.

The most obvious possibility was someone from away, a tourist, someone who had come to stay at the Sand Dollar.

"So," Doris asked. "Have you met anyone interesting lately? Guests? Visitors?"

Mercedes laughed.

"Are you kidding? I've had couples with kids—

badly, badly, badly behaved kids, I might add." Cuddling Emily, she said, "Not at all like you, angel."

"And?" Doris pleaded, not above playing the guilt card herself. "Please, Mercedes, you need to entertain me."

"There's nothing to entertain you with. It's the summer. Kids covered in damp sand, mothers just barely coping, fathers screaming at the kids *I told you not to go out so far* and then watching as they go out farther."

"Not a single interesting person?" Doris knew how to be persistent; she had lived with the teenage Tonika.

"Honestly, Doris, I'm not sure a single interesting person has arrived on the Sunshine Coast all summer. And if they have, I haven't met them."

Doris could see that Mercedes wanted to help entertain her—she could almost see the wheels rotating in her head—but what Doris looked for, Mercedes was unable to supply, perhaps because Doris refused to articulate it. If she did, Mercedes would clam up even further.

But Doris knew Mercedes, knew that she would avoid talking about this person, this lust, because she would feel it unimportant, even selfish compared to Tonika's problems. And Mercedes never liked to talk about herself.

Doris shook her head to clear it. That was untrue; Doris was projecting her own concerns onto Mercedes.

Unlike Doris, Mercedes had no trouble showing herself to the world. In fact, Doris often thought Mercedes too open about her feelings, especially about her feelings toward Doris.

Mercedes never hid the fact that she believed Doris's self-imposed serene face was a fake. And that Doris should give it up and *let it all hang out*. Mercedes was too young to have really experienced the sixties but she used the phrase to aggravate Doris.

And it worked, though she had never once given Mercedes the pleasure of seeing so.

But now? Now Doris was being forced around to Mercedes's point of view. The world—Emily and Tonika and the torture chamber—were conspiring to make her *let it all hang out*. No matter what she did, how hard she tried to hang on to her almost seven decades of training, Doris's emotions were beginning to show on her face.

Following the path to Mercedes's secret man was one of the few ways Doris felt able to return to her own self. She waited for the answer.

"Sorry, hon," Mercedes finally said, "you'll have to talk to Rose. I don't meet 'em, I just clean up after 'em."

So Doris tried Rose the next time she came by. She waited until Rose had settled in the rocking chair with

Emily, waited until the slightly stressed expression that so often marred her face these days had vanished into a haze of baby bliss.

"What is up with Mercedes?" she asked without preamble.

"Nothing," Rose replied, rocking the baby and oblivious to all else.

"Yes," Doris insisted. "Something is wrong. Or right," she said, suddenly feeling unsure of which.

"It's just the weddings."

"It is more than the weddings. More than the summer. More than envy."

"Isn't that enough?"

Doris watched Rose bend over Emily's head and wondered again why she and Sam had not had children of their own. Rose would be the kind of mother Doris wished she had been.

"Of course it is enough," Doris snapped, more because of her wayward thoughts than because of Rose's question. "It is enough but it is not all. Something more is bothering Mercedes. It is a man."

"A man?"

Rose laughed. "Doris, please. There is no man. I'd know. We'd all know. Even if Mercedes hid it from us—and why would she?—someone would tell me."

Doris sighed. And then smiled. If Rose had known of the man, had spoken his name, admitted his existence, Doris would lose her distraction. This was better.

For the first time since the arrival of the devices of torture, Doris looked forward to her sleepless night.

The man must be in Gibsons or at least between the town and Tonika's home. Mercedes had no time to go anywhere else. Although he might be a visitor. She would begin with what she could.

She would make a list and then she would call in her sources at the *Sunshine Coast News*.

Doris would find Mercedes's man. It was her project. And she always got her man.

CHAPTER 10

Doris was definitely up to something. All three of us were snoops and everyone knew it. Neither Rose nor I made the slightest attempt to hide our nosiness, but Doris? She was absolutely not drop-dead subtle. She didn't even head in the direction of subtle. Except today.

Today she was elusive. Clearly, Mrs. Doris Suzuki wasn't herself.

Under normal circumstances, the conversation we'd just had would more likely have gone like this.

Doris: You have been seeing—(insert name)—on the beach each morning for days. You have even shared your coffee with him.

Me: So?

Doris: So? What are you thinking? He is not right for you.

Me: Why not?

I asked this question not because I really wanted to

know but because conversations with Doris couldn't be changed. She was always in control and my part in them preordained.

Doris: Because he is—(insert any one of a number of things, including he's married, he's too young, too old, too fat, too thin, too rich, too poor, too many kids, too ugly, too handsome, from away)—the list was endless and easy for me to compile because I had been thinking all of the same things about my mystery man.

Doris: Mercedes, you are worth more than this. Wait. The right man will appear.

But when? I wanted to ask. I was almost fifty and he was still missing.

I hadn't even come close to finding him. There was no short list of qualified candidates. There was not a single name to go on the list.

Doris must have known that, but I was giving off some vibe she was picking up on. And Doris was more than capable of finding out his identity before I did. Mostly because I wasn't looking.

Even now, at home with Emily and Tonika, her coast telegraph worked better than mine and Rose's combined.

But this was the first time it was aimed my way. And I wasn't at all sure I liked it.

I wanted Mr. X to remain just that—a voice and a pair of hands. That way he couldn't disappoint me and I couldn't disappoint him. In my mind, that made for the perfect relationship.

The only kind of relationship—if you could call it that—that had ever worked for me.

I had, before this spring, believed that Julie would have the same bad luck as me. Oh, not that I'd ever been in love, certainly not with Julie's father. And certainly if I'd been in love and it was an unrequited passion, I'd have given it up long before Julie would have.

But still, Julie was more than old enough to have had plenty of relationships. And, until Ron, they'd all been bad. Just like her mother's.

I'd given up men almost ten years earlier as my fortieth birthday present to myself. I gave myself peace and quiet. And a great deal less aggravation.

It wasn't men in general. I had plenty of great friends who were men. But add sex to friendship and you had the big bang—and not in a good way.

Nope. Mercedes Jones and men did not mix. Never did. Never would.

But that wasn't going to keep me from the beach. I figured I had a few days before Doris figured out where I had met Mr. X and started digging into his identity. Her sources had been slowed a little bit because of the summer and her absence from the Way-Inn and the paper.

Besides, I thought as I walked down the beach the next morning, thermos in hand, I might never hear that voice again.

Really. That's exactly what I was thinking.

I wasn't hoping he'd be there before me so I could turn around and walk away before he saw me.

I wasn't wishing that he looked just like Sam Elliott in *Roadhouse*, with a face and body to match his voice and hands.

I wasn't planning this morning last night when I put out a new hot-pink T-shirt, matching sneakers and white shorts.

I wasn't watching the Weather Channel to make sure it didn't forecast rain.

I definitely didn't stop at the IGA and buy the best coffee they had in stock.

I wasn't thinking about him at all. Not for a moment.

I knew I was lying to myself but I kept doing it.

"I've done this every morning for weeks. It makes my day bearable. Why stop now?"

These words and various combinations of them accompanied me on my route down the beach. I slowed down almost to a crawl, unsure whether I wanted to see his face. I didn't know him. I'd have recognized that voice if I'd ever heard it before.

If I didn't know him, it meant he was from away. And that was a problem in all sorts of ways.

Before I'd given up men ten years earlier, I had sort of specialized for a few years in men from away. There'd been two reasons for that.

One was that there were no men on the Sunshine Coast. The only possibilities at the time had been Gray MacInnis, owner, editor and all-around everything of the *Sunshine Coast News*. Nice guy, attractive, but not even the slightest spark between us. Or Ron, the new police officer. Sweet, baby-faced and more than a little too young. Not to mention the fact that the minute she saw him, my daughter Julie fell so hard for him she'd never gotten up.

The second reason was that men from away were safe. They lived somewhere else so they couldn't interfere in my nice, comfortable life. And I didn't have to see them very often.

The problem with men from away seemed to be that every one of them wanted to give up their old life and, although this was never spoken out loud, let me look after them.

After half a dozen experiences like that, and given

the dearth of men on the Sunshine Coast, I gave them up completely. No one had come close to changing my mind. Until now.

"Wait a minute," I muttered, coming to a dead stop on the beach, spilling hot coffee from my cup onto my hands. "Damn."

The sky stretched away forever as I carefully shook the coffee from my hand to the beach instead of wiping it on my shirt or shorts as normal. The water curved up to meet the sky, its blue-gray sheen the perfect accompaniment to the brilliant clear color of the sky. No designer would put those colors together, only nature or a great painter would see their affinity.

How did he know *my* name?

If he wasn't from away, why didn't I know him?

What was I doing?

The sea and sky, as if realizing they were unable to work their usual calming magic, turned angry. It happened, even in the summer. A squall, a summer storm, a natural result of the prevailing westerlies and pretty much unpredictable.

I stood, mesmerized, unable to move as I watched the sky turn dark and the water begin to churn beneath it. The clouds, pushed by a chilly wind, moved toward me, fast and furious. The sheen of the water vanished into dull gray waves tipped with bright whitecaps, the water whipped into a frenzy by the wind.

I dropped the thermos at my feet and held out my arms. The wind promised rain, a rare treat in this month. And I could smell it coming, a clean earth-free scent, not a single molecule of dirt or flower or animal in it. Only salt and air and the deep-blue aroma of the ocean itself.

I'd always believed that the wind off the ocean had a smell, one that went further than just salt and sea. Now I stood silent on the beach and drew it into my lungs.

It smelled of distance, of loneliness, of monsoons and swirling winds and water. It smelled of ice and fire. It rang with the smell of snow-capped mountains, of heights beyond imagining. Before it arrived on my beach, this wind had tasted some of the loneliest and least-known parts of the world. And more than anything else, it smelled of the deep.

I closed my eyes against the sting of the wind. When I opened them, I saw riffling on the surface of the water.

"Five minutes," I said to the wind. "The rain will be here soon."

I sat down on the damp sand, ignoring the clean clothes I'd just moments ago tried to protect, and I opened my mouth to the wind.

I swallowed it, that deep lonely air, took it into myself, savored its emptiness and the clean taste of it.

And then I laughed at myself, a middle-aged woman suffering severe attacks of longing, sitting on the damp sand in the early morning, tasting the wind.

With the laughter came the reality.

"It's freezing out here," I screamed at the ocean. "It's July, you idiot. It's not supposed to be cold."

A warm hand touched my shoulder, then dropped an equally warm jacket over my shoulders.

"If you're going to watch a storm, you should be prepared."

I pulled the jacket around my body and added that scent to the voice and the hands. The jacket smelled of woodsmoke and salt, like bonfires on the beach on cool autumn nights. And something else.

The jacket smelled like—I took a deep breath—it smelled like sadness.

I couldn't tell you why or how I knew that, but I did.

"Where's the coffee?"

He had hunkered down on the beach right behind me, so close I felt the heat of him even through the jacket.

"Mercedes?"

"Here," I said, handing him the thermos over my shoulder. "I got distracted by the storm and dropped it."

"Don't blame you." The voice resonated through my back. "I love them myself, especially in the summer when they're so rare.

"Good coffee, and I thank you. Never really got the hang of it myself."

I knew he was walking away but I didn't turn. Instead I watched the storm and lifted my face to the rain, my body safe and warm inside his jacket.

Maybe Doris would try to find out who he was, but I wouldn't.

Not yet.

CHAPTER 11

Mercedes knew just what to do. She always knew what to do.

Well, Rose used to be like that and pretty soon she was going to be like that again.

She hoped.

"For the next couple of nights," Mercedes said, pulling a bottle from her pocket, "take these."

"Valerian?"

"It's an herbal sleep aid. Non-addictive. Just helps you stop fretting so you can sleep."

Rose wanted to ask Mercedes why she carried valerian in her pocket but she got distracted when she opened the bottle and a couple of capsules spilled into her hand.

"Ewwww," she screamed. "These smell awful."

Unable to resist, even though she knew the result, she lifted her hand to her nose.

"Mercedes, these smell like…shit. I couldn't swallow them if I hadn't slept for ten years."

Mercedes laughed. "Hold your nose, okay? And wash your hands after you take them. They'll help. I promise."

Mercedes disappeared before Rose got a chance to ask why she carried the capsules in her pocket. She'd try to remember to ask her later but it probably didn't matter. You never knew with Mercedes—she might have picked them up for someone at the Sand Dollar or saw them at the pharmacy and thought they were interesting.

That was the thing about Mercedes, Rose thought. She was interested in everything and she had no hesitation about trying new things. Rose admired her for that.

She knew the valerian wasn't all of the solution Mercedes had in mind. She hoped that the rest of the idea smelled better than the first part.

The valerian did work, at least a bit. She managed to increase her sleep hours from five to six, which put her right on the edge of okay. At least for sleep.

But it didn't stop the fretting. And since Sam slept like he did everything else, with enthusiasm, she still had at least two hours a night to lie in bed and worry.

Because the only thing that could wake Sam once he was asleep was the absence of Rose.

"I want you to go, Rose-babe," he'd say when she told him about a trip to the city with Doris and Mercedes that she'd decided not to take. She knew, and he knew, that he wouldn't sleep a single minute while she was gone.

So her trips without Sam were limited to overnight. The minute she walked back in the door—morning, noon or night—he hauled her up the stairs. He'd fall into the bed, Rose in his arms, and he'd be asleep before he'd kissed Rose hello.

Rose couldn't go to the living room and turn on the TV. She couldn't surf the Web. She could read a book but she wasn't yet ready to admit that her sleeping woes were permanent. Somehow putting a separate reading lamp on her side of the bed would mean acknowledging a problem that couldn't be solved.

So she waited for Mercedes and her solution, repeating the words, *six weeks, it's only six weeks,* to herself in the late afternoon when the lack of sleep turned her into a drone. She was an almost-lighter-than-air drone but that didn't make any difference at all to her drone-ness.

For the first time in years, Rose carried a pen and a pad in her apron.

"Can I take your order?" she asked Rowena Dale, who'd been ordering the exact same tuna fish on brown with extra dill pickles every afternoon for at least twenty years. Probably longer, but someone else had taken those orders.

Rowena looked at the pen and paper, at Rose's hand holding them, and then up at Rose's face.

"You're kidding, right? Paying me back for the last cancelled engagement party."

Rose shrugged.

"No," she said, "I'm tired, don't want to make any mistakes."

Rowena lifted Rose's skirt up to her thighs.

"Rowena," she whispered. "What are you doing?"

Rose pushed down her skirt but it was too late.

The bruises on her thighs glowed like dark beacons in the sunlight; Rose had lost her grace along with her ability to sleep. She banged into counters and tables. She tripped over carpets, snagged her sweaters on sharp edges—edges she'd been successfully avoiding for years—and ruined all her shoes by banging the toes and heels into hitherto avoidable obstacles.

Her clothes, and her body, were a mess.

Rowena might be pushing eighty but she had eyes like a hawk and a mind as sharp as, well, Rose couldn't think of anyone to compare to Rowena.

"You're more than just tired, girl. You're losing it."

Satisfied, Rowena settled back in the booth with her paper, leaving Rose wavering between laughter and tears. She thought that a good combination. Recently there had been no laughter involved.

Rowena wasn't the only regular who noticed the change in Rose. The only ones who didn't were the soon-to-be newlyweds but she didn't see much of them anyway. When she did, they were too busy ogling each other to worry about their burgers or beer being late or lukewarm.

Rose suffered through some variation on Rowena's theme half a dozen times a day, though few of them were as blunt—or as dismissive—as Rowena.

"Are you okay, sweetie?" the men asked, patting her carefully on the shoulder and nodding amiably when she said, "I'm fine."

The women took a little more convincing.

"I'm worried about you, Rose." Then, looking around furtively and lowering their voices, they'd continue, "Are you pregnant?"

Rose laughed at the idea and the questioner but being asked it over and over again made her even more nervous. Nervous enough to travel to Sechelt on her way home from Doris and Emily's to buy a home pregnancy test, thus giving the rumors more impetus.

She'd felt safe in the big drugstore in Sechelt, but of course she knew the cashier and all three of the customers in line with her.

Rose cursed herself as she watched the tiny paddle confirm her non-pregnantness. She had known she wasn't, couldn't be pregnant but she was unable to believe in her own self anymore.

Rose began to run out of metaphors to describe her state. Cracked egg, cracked ceiling, orbiter. Now she thought about a kite being bounced around at the whim of the wind.

"At least," she said to the sleeping Sam that night, "at least my metaphors are consistent. Two cracking, two lighter than air. Maybe now I can move on to something else."

Sam snored in reply. Most times, Rose let that sound lull her to sleep, knowing she was exactly where she wanted to be. Now it was just one more aggravation.

The morning after the pregnancy-test fiasco, Rose phoned Mercedes.

No answer.

"No answer?" she said to Sam. "Where is she? It's six o'clock in the morning."

Sam smiled at her over the top of his newspaper. He always smiled at her.

"In the shower?"

"She never showers until she's finished cleaning the rooms."

"Maybe someone's got an early check-out."

"No. Mercedes doesn't open the office until half an hour before that early ferry during the week. And no one goes home on that early ferry except on a Monday."

Sam patted her shoulder and moved on, following his regular morning routine, oblivious to her anxiety. He puttered in the bedroom, then the bathroom, then the hallway. In the mornings, Rose thought, Sam reminded her of her father. He didn't put on a suit or a tie—more likely a Hawaiian shirt and Bermuda shorts and it didn't matter whether it was July or January—but it took him twice as long as Rose to get ready.

Mostly, she thought, the puttering and the resemblance to her father were just more things she loved about Sam.

Today, though, today they made her angry. More than angry, today Sam made her furious.

And that, Rose thought, was the final straw, the one that broke the camel's back, the one that covered the needle in the haystack, the one that…

Well, the one that made her crave Mercedes. Because if Rose was angry at Sam, all the valerian in the world wasn't going to be enough. Rose had moved far past fretting, far past losing it. She'd crossed the line into pure unadulterated craziness.

And the only person who could save her—and Rose wasn't sure how she knew this—was Mercedes.

"Sam," she called through the bathroom door, "I'm going to the Sand Dollar."

"Right now?"

"Yes." And then Rose did something she'd never done before with Sam; she'd never told him even the smallest of little white lies.

"I'm worried about Mercedes. It's not like her not to answer her phone."

The door swung open.

"Did you want me to come with you?"

Rose's anger vanished in a heartbeat. But she persisted in the lie.

"No. I'm sure it's just me worrying for nothing. I'll be right back."

She hurried from the room before her expression gave her away. Except, of course, Sam would put it down to worry about Mercedes and not to anything being wrong with Rose.

"I can't believe I lied to Sam."

Mercedes reached out and touched Rose's forehead. "You sure you don't have a fever?"

Rose shook her head. She'd rushed through the

storm to the Sand Dollar, the rain blowing cool in her face. She felt the chill right through her skin to her bones and into the marrow. Even if she did have a fever, the wind would have blown it away.

Mercedes poured a cup of coffee and put it into Rose's shaking hands.

"Here, hon, hold on to this. It'll warm you up."

And then Mercedes did the thing Rose had always loved her for. She sat down across the table and she glowed. It was, Rose thought, as if she had learned a way to intensify her ability to listen, but it was more than that. When Mercedes glowed, she heard not only the words but what the words were hiding. And she heard the silence as well.

She didn't do it very often and she'd never done it with Rose—this was a day full of firsts and it wasn't yet seven o'clock—but Rose had seen the glow half a dozen times over the past twenty years. She understood what it meant.

Each time, a problem had been uncovered. Rose suspected that it wasn't about solutions but about knowledge. Mercedes's other faces—the glow and the goddess of justice—were opposing faces of a single idea. Knowledge and action. Rose needed the knowledge. She'd work out the action herself.

Or she would if she—or Mercedes—could ever figure out the problem.

"So," Mercedes said, her glow warming the room with a soft golden light, "you lied to Sam."

"I told him I had to come to the Sand Dollar because I was worried about you."

"Were you?"

"A little." Rose felt her face scrunch into an expression of concern. "Where were you?"

"On the beach. Why'd you lie to Sam?"

Rose tried to deflect the question.

"I've never, not once in the past twenty-five years, lied to Sam. Not even a little white lie, the kind my mother said was okay. You know, saying I like your hat even when it's terrible, or your child is beautiful even when it's as ugly as a banana slug."

"What's different today?"

"I've never been mad at him either."

"No?"

Mercedes sounded disbelieving and Rose wasn't surprised. Mercedes was often angry—at suppliers, at people who mistreated their dogs, at the government. Almost always at the government.

"Not this kind of mad, not the kind of mad that makes you want to walk out the door and never come back. And especially not over something he's done every day of our life together."

"But you are going back."

Mercedes said those words without the slightest shadow of doubt coloring them and Rose loved her for that as well.

"It's not about Sam," Rose replied after a few moments' thought. "It's about me."

"You're kidding, right? Of course it's about you. What we're trying to get out is what. What is it?"

"I don't know. It's not the baby. It's not Sam. It's not the summer."

"Turning forty?"

"But why? Forty is the new thirty and I loved turning thirty."

"It *is* the baby," Mercedes said. "I saw you watching that young man the other day. You looked like I feel."

Rose risked a quick glance at Mercedes as the glow faded. Even as she watched, she saw Mercedes square her shoulders and the glow strengthen again.

"Mercedes?" she asked, slightly frightened and even more concerned that she'd gained something else to worry about.

"It's nothing, Rose. Really. I'm just thinking about Julie and all we have to do before September. Why couldn't she wait to get married until November? Or December? September's a terrible month."

Now Rose may have been obsessed with her own worries but she knew Mercedes well enough to know that, while she may have been worried about Julie, that wasn't why the glow faded. She also knew her well enough to ignore that knowledge. The glow was directed at Rose and there was no way Rose would waste it.

She tucked the worry into the back of her mind, crowded with scores of other things stacked there, things she'd put away to deal with at a better time. At this rate, she thought, she'd never get to them. She kept adding and never subtracting.

"What does it feel like?" Mercedes asked.

"What does *what* feel like?"

"The thing," Mercedes said, "the thing that's got you tied up in knots, the thing that's hiding in that black hole in your stomach. The thing—" the glow intensified "—you don't want to think about."

"Oh," Rose said. "That thing."

She sat back in the chair and realized that as soon as Mercedes had asked, she'd known she would be able to figure out what it was. She reached past the justifications to the black hole. She hadn't known she had one until Mercedes mentioned it, still wasn't a hundred percent convinced of it, but if the glowing Mercedes said it was there, Rose was willing to try it.

She dug past all sorts of things.

Past Sam.

Past Doris, Tonika and Emily.

Past Mercedes.

"Rose," Mercedes interrupted. "This is about you, not anyone else. I know you're worried about everyone else, but this thing is about you."

Rose thought about that for a minute, then nodded. Mercedes was right, but Rose knew the way her mind worked. She'd have to acknowledge the others before she could get past them.

She started again and worked her way past other things.

Past the hermit.

Past the weddings.

Past the baby.

That was a big one and Rose wasn't sure that it wasn't *the one*. She thought about it.

"I really want to see my son," she said. "I want to make sure he's all right, that he has everything he needs."

"It's not just that," Mercedes said, certainty in her voice.

"It isn't?"

"No. Even if this other thing isn't at the root of your problem, it's bothering you much more than you're admitting."

"It is?"

Rose's faith in Mercedes was tested. She thought she'd dealt with the baby thing, had been dealing with it every day for a quarter of a century. She struggled to dig deeper into her feelings about her son, the one thing she'd felt positive about through the whole summer. She'd figured out it was bugging her and she'd dealt with it. She'd contacted the adoption agency and put herself on the willing-to-be-contacted list. There was nothing else she could do. Or was there?

"A private investigator?" she asked.

"Maybe," Mercedes replied. "But that's not what I'm talking about. I'm talking about you. Of course you want to know how he is. But why now? What's pushing you?"

Rose shrugged. "I don't know, but I am going to think about hiring someone to look for him."

Mercedes's face turned solemn and Rose knew what she would say next. She stopped Mercedes and said it herself, said the thing she'd been trying to ignore. She pulled it from where she'd buried it deep in the darkest closet in the basement of her mind. She unlocked the five locks, threw back the deadbolts at top and bottom, pulled out the iron bar that held it shut at the bottom, and wrenched open the rusted-shut door.

"I need to make sure he isn't dead."

CHAPTER 12

The torture continued, as did the tears. The only happy person in the house was Emily, and Doris envied her.

She wondered whether it was a baby thing, but she remembered that Tonika had been serious, both as a baby and as a child. She seldom cried, but also seldom laughed, so Doris had nothing to compare Emily's cheerfulness to, no way to measure whether it was just Emily. Perhaps, she thought, it was a response to the pain around her?

Doris hoped not and chose, eventually, to see it as Emily's sunny personality. Everyone loved her smiling face. She even managed to make Doris smile through her tears at the end of yet another impossible day.

Each morning, Doris woke dreading the day before her. The sun shone in her window and she wished for gray skies. The birds sang and she cursed them. She wanted the world outside to reflect more accurately the world inside her.

Even the assistance of Rose and Mercedes was not enough to lift the despair enveloping her.

Doris was no longer sure she could do it. Two weeks into Tonika's physio regime and Doris was just barely getting by. It was not the physical work—in fact, that seemed to be having a positive effect. She felt stronger, her arthritis less painful, her breathing steadier.

That did not seem to be so for Tonika. She seemed to be in far more pain than when she began.

Each day, Doris asked the head torturer whether that could be right.

"She cannot sleep," she'd say, "not even with the sleeping pills. Her leg aches. No," she'd say, considering, "I think it is more like shooting pains. Sometimes in the night she screams."

Doris did not have any real evidence about Tonika's pain because Tonika never spoke about it. She inferred this pain from the look on Tonika's face, from the moaning when she was forced from her bed to the rack, from the lacklustre way she sometimes looked at Emily, as if even a smile were too much for her.

The physiotherapist looked sympathetic when she replied, but Doris did not trust that sympathy. The look was probably learned in school along with the torture.

"The therapy isn't easy," she said, a practiced smile on her face, "but it is necessary."

"Perhaps we should rethink the program?" Doris asked as politely as a question like that could be asked. "Perhaps a different method?"

"All her doctors have seen and approved the program. Mrs. Suzuki—" the torturer took Doris's hand and led her to the sofa "—maybe this work is too much for you. I'm sure I could find…"

"No, no." Doris panicked. "I can do it. I am just worried about my daughter's pain."

But it was really the emotional effect that Doris had trouble dealing with. And that, Doris thought, was an understatement.

She wanted to wear a blindfold and ear plugs each time she stepped into the living room with Tonika. She could not bear the look on her daughter's face as she pushed herself past the limits of her endurance. She could not listen to her pain-filled voice saying, "Again, Mama, we have to do it again."

Only two things managed to pierce the gloom.

Emily's laugh cut right through the veil and lightened the day until it became almost bearable. Not quite bearable, though. What made the day bearable was the mystery.

Mercedes. And her man. Who was he? Where had she met him? Where did she see him?

In the afternoons, when she used to nap, while Emily and Tonika still did, Doris followed the mystery. She was discreet. And careful. She was determined to solve this herself, so was especially careful to give no clues as to what she really searched for, no hints of who she wondered about.

Of course her informants knew something was up but after a few questions without response, they stopped asking and just answered Doris's questions. They knew the secret would be public knowledge one day and they could then take credit for a job well done. Doris had counted on this.

She began, as always, with Rowena Dale. Rowena had lived her entire eighty years on the Sunshine Coast. She could have been a charter member of the gossip queens if she weren't so engrossed in her quest for a husband. Rowena Dale, acerbic, quick-witted and curious, often knew more things and sooner than the gossip queens.

She shared this knowledge only with Doris and for this, especially now, Doris was grateful.

"Rowena. How are you?"

Doris began slowly and carefully and in the most roundabout way she could devise.

"What am I missing?" she asked. "I know it is summer but still things are happening."

"Damn, Doris, you haven't missed a thing except Julie and Ron practically swooning over each other. They're treating Gibsons like it's Paris—kissing all over the place. Right in public. At least they don't do it when he's on duty."

A hum came from the phone line, a hum which Doris knew meant that Rowena was considering.

"No, let me rephrase that. They don't do it when he's on duty and anyone can see them. I bet they do, though, I just bet they do."

"I am happy to hear that they are discreet. It would show great disrespect for the RCMP and I'm sure Ron would be conscious of the respect to be shown to them."

"Sure, sure. Josie Harris and Gray MacInnis are much more careful. They only kiss in the office…"

Doris gasped; she could not help herself. "In the office? At the *Sunshine Coast News*? That cannot be right."

"Oh, they're pretty careful, but not quite careful enough. Still, there's nothing wrong with either of them—it's just got me kinda hot under the collar."

Doris laughed politely. Rowena's obsessive search for a husband had always seemed a bit ridiculous to her.

Once Mr. Suzuki had died, Doris had been perfectly content without a man.

"I still do not think kissing in public—except perhaps in Paris—can be a good thing. But it was to be expected," she said. "They are young and in love."

Rowena laughed, her deep voice booming over the phone lines. That was another reason Doris had called Rowena—she had such a loud voice, Doris never had to strain to hear her.

"At least they're young and think they're in love. I don't know how you can tell. Not really."

Neither did Doris, but leading the conversation in that direction would be unprofitable.

"What else have I missed?" she asked. "Any newcomers?"

There were sure to be some. Every summer at least one of the visitors decided they had to live on the Sunshine Coast full-time.

"It's not a long commute," they'd say, ignoring the realities of a forty-five-minute ferry ride each way, the cost of the trip, the waiting time, the possibilities of storms and delays. The lengthy drive at one or both ends seemed to be irrelevant in the heat of their tourist passion.

It was like love at first sight. It was like being a teenager, or at least as Doris had observed it, not as she had experienced it. Intense passion, unrestrainable passion. You wanted. You had to have. You did whatever it took to get the object of your passion, whether that object was good for you or not. That was how tourists felt about the Sunshine Coast.

The newcomers generally bought a house from someone who had experienced the exact same passion two or three years earlier. And so the cycle continued. Only a very small percentage of newcomers stayed long enough to become members of the community, and those were almost always the ones who were retired or found themselves a way to make a living on the peninsula.

"Only two couples," Rowena said. "One of them bought that vacant house right by the terminal."

"They will not stay long," Doris said.

"Nope. That house has been bought and sold every summer since it was built. Maybe it's haunted."

Doris ignored that direction as well and persevered on her chosen path.

"Who are they?"

"Very young. They're brokers, I think. Fancy clothes, fancy cars, two fancy dogs just the right size to drop-kick."

"How young?"

"You expect me to know? Very young. They look like teenagers to me. Oh, and I forgot to tell you—" Rowena paused for effect and Doris knew she had not forgotten, had just waited for the right moment "—they're both women."

"Oh," Doris replied. "How interesting. Will they stay over the winter?"

"Don't know. Don't care. They don't come to the Way-Inn, seem to be keeping pretty much to themselves."

"Who are the others?"

"They bought one of them hotshot condos up the way. You know, the ones Marlene and Fred used to live in. Pretty sure they moved into Marlene's condo now she's off cruising."

That sounded much more promising. That building, although not officially age-restricted, had attracted older people. No really young couples, definitely no children.

"They are retired?"

"I think so. Close, anyway. She's tall and thin and brown as a surfer which, for all I know, she might be."

"What about him?"

"He's a leprechaun."

Doris had no idea what Rowena meant by that. It could mean many things. He could be Irish or rich or his skin might have a faint green tinge. He might have moved in with a pot of gold under his arm. She settled for a noncommittal grunt and waited.

"He's about five feet tall, half a head—the bottom half—of bright red hair and he bounces around like a tennis ball. He's gotta be eighty if he's a day," she said disparagingly.

Doris smiled to herself. Rowena Dale, eighty herself, watched other octogenarians with an eagle eye. If they did not live up to her standard of health and exuberance, they were letting down the side. Obviously, the leprechaun did not make the grade.

Doris ignored the disappointment she felt at the description of the couple and pressed on.

"That is it? The whole summer we have had only two sets of newcomers?"

"What can I say? It's been a slow year—mostly young families and a whole bunch of bikers."

"Cyclists? I have not seen any."

"No. Bikers. Hogs. Harleys. Big fat guys and tall skinny guys and motorcycle mamas. All with tattoos and long hair."

Doris heard the interest in Rowena's voice and wondered whether her next fiancé would be a biker.

"Oh, those kinds of bikers. Anyone interesting coming to the writers' festival? I have lost my schedule."

Doris assumed she had received one; everyone on the peninsula was automatically on the mailing list.

But she might have simply thrown it away without a glance, as she had done with a fair number of bills for which she was now receiving late notices.

"This year is mostly non-fiction and women."

That stopped Doris in her tracks and besides, she realized, it would have to be someone who worked for the festival. The authors would not arrive for another three weeks.

"It sounds like I have missed very little?" She made that statement sound like a question.

"You've missed nothing except Rose and Mercedes acting like fools."

"What?"

Doris's mother would have slapped her hand for such an abrupt and rude question but it had flown out of her mouth before she could stop it.

"Rose has bruises all over her legs from banging into things and she can't remember my lunch order—even though I've been having exactly the same thing for twenty years."

"I know there is something bothering her," Doris said. "I suspect she is unhappy about turning forty."

Rowena's harsh bark of laughter echoed Doris's thoughts. Forty was young, far too young to be worrying over.

"What about Mercedes?" Doris asked. "She seems her normal self to me."

Doris pondered the ethics of that little white lie. Mercedes did not seem normal to her at all. She seemed—what? Distracted, maybe. Of course she was busy and the summer always made everyone a bit frazzled, but this summer, Mercedes was distracted.

"Maybe so, but there's something." Rowena laughed again. "Can't quite put my finger on it. Don't see her much in the summer, not like Rose, so maybe she was just having a bad day."

Doris smiled to herself at this confirmation of her idea about Mercedes. There *was* something to find out, something to know.

"Thank you, Rowena, you have cheered me immensely. Perhaps we will talk again soon."

Doris bounced in her chair with glee. No, she had not solved the mystery but she had confirmation that there was a mystery to solve. She would consider her next move this evening.

It would keep her mind occupied while she tortured her daughter on that vile metal device. It would help her keep her face still and her eyes tear-free while she pushed Tonika to and then past her limits.

It would allow Doris to keep doing what she knew

was necessary. The mystery had become essential to her sanity.

Doris stood up from the chair and moved away from the phone, which felt like a lifeline. It would still be there tomorrow.

CHAPTER 13

Instead of getting easier as the season progressed, as I got used to the long hours and hard work, as I got used to dealing with cranky strangers and screaming children, this summer just got more and more difficult.

Rose's problem was unsolvable. Nothing she nor I could do would change anything. So she'd have to wait. And wait. And maybe she'd never know.

There was no way I could do that, no way I was capable of waiting for an answer that might never arrive. No wonder Rose was falling apart. I thought she was dealing with it as well as possible. Me, I'd probably be drinking my way into oblivion.

I needed to talk to Doris about Rose even though I knew the conversation might make my situation more complicated. I bit the bullet and picked up the phone.

"Doris?"

"Mercedes. Why are you calling me so early?"

Oops. I'd forgotten that not everyone walked the beach at dawn. More ammunition for Mrs. Snoop.

"Sorry. I've been up for a while. Busy week and I've been worrying about Rose."

I *had* been worrying about her, just not this morning.

"Oh?"

Doris Suzuki at her most disbelieving. I hated it when she used that tone of voice. Damn.

"She's not herself this summer and I've finally figured out why. I don't know what to do about it," I said to Doris.

"She is concerned that her son is dead. We need to hire someone to find him, whether he is dead or alive. Only once she knows for certain will she begin to get better."

I didn't know why I was surprised. Of course Doris knew what was wrong and of course she had already figured out the solution.

"I was going to talk to you about this today," she continued, "at a reasonable hour. You will know better than I where to find someone to undertake this research."

I glanced at my watch.

"It's eight o'clock," I protested. "This *is* a reasonable hour."

"For you perhaps, but no one in this house is sleeping very well."

I apologized, thinking of the strain I'd seen on

Tonika's face yesterday. She might be getting stronger but it was taking a huge toll on all of them.

She'd inherited that indomitable will from Doris and nothing would stop either of them. Tonika would push herself as far and as hard as it took, pulling Doris and Richard along with her. I didn't know how Doris stood it.

Yes, I did. She managed as she did with everything—she firmed up her face, she dismissed every negative thought, and then she lived her life as if that life were perfect.

She had lived her life that way for almost seventy years, burying anything that might spoil the image of that complete serenity. But that serenity had to crack sometime and this summer it had happened. It had been evident in her tears, in her shaking hands and the way she'd accepted—without real protest—our help with Emily and Tonika.

I wished we, I, could do more, but both Rose and I were already stretched to our limits. And how odd was that? That all three of us were living the summer from hell?

Not odd at all. We often seemed to run our lives along parallel tracks. Not the same, but similar, something about our closeness, about our ages, about our lives.

And my envy of Julie? My undirected lust and

longing? My problems were nothing compared to Doris's and Rose's, but they were still there. My nice, even, organized life was falling apart, just as their lives were.

But the phone calls about the wedding had slowed to a manageable level as the arrangements got settled. One less stress.

I still had trouble seeing Julie and Ron together, but it wasn't that hard to avoid seeing them more than once or twice a day. And then mostly from a distance.

I was running flat out between the Sand Dollar and Doris's, with the occasional stop at the Way-Inn to check on Rose.

Don't get me wrong—I loved my daughter—but it still wasn't easy to watch the two of them together. Harder, actually, now my longing had an object.

Anyway, Doris needed help I couldn't give her. Rose needed something I wasn't sure even a private investigator could find. And me? I was going to be fine. Really.

Over the past week, I'd given up walking on the beach. I didn't want to see his face and I especially didn't want to give Doris any more clues.

But I missed those walks. And I missed him.

Stupid, I knew. I'd never even seen him. Maybe it was more accurate to say that I missed the idea of him, knowing that if I turned around I would see him, and the anticipation of that moment.

Of the three of us, though, I was, as the summer progressed, the most in control. My longing, as strong as it seemed to be, was under control. Having an object—even an unknown, unseen, unrequited object—somehow made it easier to sleep, to eat, to get through the day.

But Doris and Rose? They needed *me* to be in control. They needed *me* to help them. And maybe knowing how much they needed me was what was keeping me going, just as knowing that Tonika and Emily needed her was what was keeping Doris going. I couldn't fall apart. Not now.

September might be a different story. I often fell apart in September and spent days in bed, watching home renovation shows and dreaming about paint colors. A slight fever, a cough, a bout of exhaustion—sure signs of a relaxing of my body's defences.

So, like almost everyone else on the Sunshine Coast, I started counting down the days to Labor Day, the traditional end of the summer rush. The tourists didn't stop coming after Labor Day, they just stopped coming in such large numbers. We stopped seeing parents and kids, university students and bikers who liked the sunshine and hated even the possibility of rain. We still saw retirees and older couples, but the big rush was over.

I just needed to make it through August and everything would be fine.

The next morning, I resumed my walks on the beach because there was no way I'd make it through the next month without something to look forward to.

And it wasn't about Mr. X, at least not much of it. It was about having one single hour of the day for me, Mercedes Jones. Not for work or Julie or Rose or Doris. Not for the private investigator or Emily or the wedding plans. Not for the Shelter Ball or the guests at the Sand Dollar.

One single hour just for me.

I deserved it.

I wanted it.

I needed it.

And damn it, I was going to take it.

And I wasn't going to worry about Doris and her snooping. Because I was going to turn around and find out who he was before she had a chance to track him down.

And maybe, just maybe, this morning would be the one when I'd do it, when I'd get up the nerve to turn around and see the man who knew my name and spoke it in a voice I couldn't resist.

Last week's storm had blown away every speck of dust and cloud in the sky. The clear blue shone as if it were newly painted with a bright, glossy, expensive paint created especially for this particular morning.

The world smelled clean, too, fresh and clear and sweet.

I sat down on the washed-clean rock at the very end of the point and waited. I didn't have to wait long.

A hand reached over my shoulder and grabbed the thermos.

"I've missed you this week, Mercedes Jones. And your coffee."

I hadn't been imagining the effect of that voice. It was as deep and husky and resonant as I remembered.

The hand returned the thermos over my shoulder and I heard a rustling as he sat down behind me, felt the warmth of his body not far from me.

I poured myself another cup of coffee and knew I was going to turn around. For the first time, I found myself wondering about his motives and feelings, not just mine. If he'd wanted me to see him, he would have sat beside me. And he didn't.

He hadn't made it impossible for me to discover his identity, but he had made it obvious that he didn't want me to do so.

I'd respect his wishes, though I couldn't do anything about Doris. I laughed out loud. I respected his wishes only because they echoed mine. I'd thought this morning that I'd turn around when he arrived, but I'd been wrong.

I wasn't ready.

And I might never be ready, never want to face the disillusionment I was sure would come with the discovery. Because there was no way that the man sitting quietly behind me was suitable.

I'd spent the last few weeks reviewing the men on the Sunshine Coast, considering their ages, their marital status, their physical characteristics. There was not one single man on the peninsula who might, by any stretch of even the most vivid imagination, be considered suitable for a woman my age.

Yes, there were several—okay, more than several—eligible eighty-year-olds. Nice guys, mostly. I played crib with them at the club in the winter, listened to their stories for the tenth or twentieth or thirtieth time. I liked them, but they were so frail, and I was so buff and healthy and strong from working at the Sand

Dollar that I could crush them in a moment. No passion possible.

Yes, there were, at least during the summer, quite a few young men working in the marinas and resorts and restaurants for the season. Working right along with gorgeous young babes doing the same thing.

Again, nice kids, but *kids* was the operative word. They could be my children, some of them even, with a stretch, my grandchildren.

Single men between thirty and sixty were in extremely short supply on the Sunshine Coast. In fact, there weren't any. At least not any I knew.

And I was a member of the gossip queens. I'd know. I'd know before almost anyone else on the peninsula—except for Rose, Doris and Rowena Dale, of course.

So whoever sat behind me had to be someone I didn't know but someone who knew me. Not a surprise, really. Everyone knew the gossip queens. We got pointed out in the Way-Inn as if we were a tourist attraction.

"Look," someone would say to their from-away cousins or friends or paying guests. "There's Mercedes Jones. She's one of the gossip queens."

And the recipient of this knowledge would look at me, eyes wide and mouth open, as if he or she looked at the Eiffel Tower or the Pyramids.

I was used to people coming up to me on the street and asking if I was, "Mercedes Jones? One of the gossip queens?"

"Yes," I'd say. And then, stuck at that word, I'd turn and walk away. Because what could I say to them? I took my cues from the Eiffel Tower. I stood tall and still, let them take my photograph and watched them move on to the next photo op.

I often wondered how many strangers had my picture in their holiday album labelled Gossip Queen of the Sunshine Coast. The thought entertained and worried me at the same time, but most times the entertainment won out.

Okay, so Mr. X was probably one of those strangers—someone from away, some visitor. It was possible he'd know me and I not know him. More than possible, it was likely.

He hadn't bought a house here, though, because that I would know. Only two sets of newcomers this year. Mutt and Jeff—and there was no way the leprechaun spoke like my man—and the female couple who'd bought the haunted house next to the terminal.

A visitor, but he had to be a long-term one. I'd been seeing him—metaphorically speaking—on the beach for weeks. And that was how Doris would find him, I thought, by figuring out where he could be staying. Once she figured out where I saw him she'd know he had to be staying either in or close to Gibsons.

There were dozens of motels and bed and breakfasts but Doris was persistent. Knowing a general location was all she needed to find him.

I was going to have to turn around, that was all there was to it. Even if I didn't tell Doris about him, I didn't want her to tell me.

I took a deep breath and twisted my torso until I faced the beach. And…

"Damn. Damn. Damn."

While I'd been thinking about who he might be, he'd walked away and I hadn't even heard him go.

"Tomorrow," I said, gathering up the thermos. "I'll find out who he is tomorrow."

But that didn't happen, either. The next morning I was late, the following morning it rained, the next morning he didn't show.

My patience, what little I had of it, shredded into a million tiny pieces and scattered itself all over my bedroom, the one place I felt free to rant about my bitch of a summer. With everyone I knew counting on me to solve their problems, I had little time or energy to spare for my own.

So I turned my bedroom from its usual tranquil space to the psychic equivalent of a dojo. I fought with my temper, my rapidly waning patience, my longing, the lust I kept trying to deny. I pummelled my worry into submission. I drop-kicked my exhaustion into another dimension.

I cursed and cried and screamed.

I did things I'd always wanted to do and had never allowed myself.

I took my feather pillow and banged it against the wall and the headboard and kept banging until the seams split and the feathers coated the room.

I put on my hiking boots and kicked down the door to my closet. And then I kicked matching holes in my drywall. And I didn't fix them, either.

A box of old china destined for the thrift shop got lugged from storage. I flung each piece—from mugs and tea cups to dinner plates and glasses—onto the floor, shattering them until the floor swam with sharp edges.

I played rock and roll at the highest level my stereo would go, screaming along with the Boss and the Rolling Stones.

I was careful with all of these things to make sure that any guests were out. I closed the windows, turned on the No Vacancy sign and the answering machine, and closed the curtains in all my rooms. Just in case.

No one could see Mercedes Jones breaking china or kicking holes in her walls. It would inevitably get back to Doris and Rose and neither of them needed more grief.

No, the psychic dojo was private. And it would stay that way.

CHAPTER 14

Rose sat in the back booth of the Way-Inn, her hands clasped and motionless on the table in front of her.

She hadn't moved for hours. Sam had brought her tea, but the white cup, now stained with tannin, had not been moved since he had placed it before her.

Her butt hurt and she felt the sore bones of her tailbone. These were physical reminders of the pain she felt in her heart.

She sat without moving until she felt frozen in space. If she unclasped her hands, they would not work. If she unbent her legs from beneath the table, they would not bear her weight. If she shifted on the bench, excruciating pain—a pain she felt waiting for her—would radiate out from her tailbone and up her spine to join her headache.

Rose wasn't certain whether she'd blinked her eyes even once since she'd sat down in the booth. Her eyes seemed stuck open and no tears helped moisten them.

All of this pain, Rose believed, was her penance. Not for giving up her son—she knew she'd done the only thing possible at the time—but for even contemplating the possibility that he might be dead.

The moment Mercedes had forced her to speak those words, Rose had realized what they meant.

Her son was no longer protected by her complete and unwavering belief in his existence, her knowledge of his feet on the planet, his place in this world.

Now, Rose knew, he was at risk. Because her faith, her belief in him, had kept him safe.

Rose sat in the booth and tried to get that faith back.

"He's living in the city. He's on his way to university right now." She checked her watch. "He's on the express bus. It's blue," she said, adding layers of detail to her story, "and it's one of those articulated ones. It twists around corners like a Slinky."

She barely noticed as Sam slid his bulk into the booth across from her, ignored him as he replaced the stained tea cup with a fresh one and poured a steaming cup of fragrant jasmine tea.

She did feel it, with a fierce jolt of pain, when he reached across and carefully unclasped her hands.

Rose refused to cry or even cry out, simply sat as

Sam's warm rough hands massaged hers out of the cramped position they'd locked themselves into.

"He's wearing a light jacket. Still too heavy for the summer, though. It's black. Blue jeans, faded from too many washings, and boots. Brown suede Daytons."

Sam placed the steaming cup into her hands, his two hands around hers, gently forcing the cup to her lips. He said nothing, just waited for her to take a sip.

Rose's preoccupation was broken for a few short moments as she considered, from somewhere outside her obsession, the way Sam always knew exactly what to do. She couldn't speak to him and he understood that, just worked around it.

His presence in the booth, the silence surrounding her—he must have closed the Way-Inn, she thought without surprise—seemed to make her job easier.

And she knew that Mercedes must have called Sam, must have told him what she had finally admitted. A tiny warm spot appeared in her cold heart.

She spoke, louder this time.

"He has a backpack and it's too heavy. His shoulders are wide, though, and he ignores the weight of it. He's wearing sunglasses just like the ones Keanu Reeves wore in *The Matrix*. They look good on him."

Sam nodded and helped her take another sip of tea.

"The bus is passing a McDonald's. It won't be long before he's on campus."

Rose's brow wrinkled and for the first time, she looked directly at Sam. And then she blinked, slowly, painfully shuttering her eyes. She blinked again, not quite ready to go on.

"What do you think he's taking?" she asked. "I need to know and I can't think. I didn't go to university and I don't know what he might take. Engineering? Science? Math? Computers? Everyone's taking computers. Or maybe he's taking art. Or... I just don't know."

She placed her fingers at her temples, trying to massage an answer into her brain. "Think," she said with each rotation. "You have to think."

"He's taking English," Sam said. "Look at the books in his backpack. It's obvious."

Rose looked up, not even surprised that Sam knew the answer.

"Of course. Chaucer. No wonder the backpack weighs a ton. Joseph Conrad. Virginia Woolf. Al Purdy."

It made sense to her. Books were her only passion. Next to Sam, of course. Her son—she tried to forget that she didn't know his name—inherited his love of books from her.

"I hated Chaucer," she said. "I liked the stories but

I couldn't learn Middle English. I couldn't learn any other language."

"But you took French in high school."

"Never learned more than menus and the backs of cereal boxes. It was my worst subject."

Rose went back to work. If she imagined him—she refused to think the word *alive*—in his regular life, she thought, he would be fine.

"I need to use the computer," she said, trying to stand and falling back into the booth when her legs collapsed beneath her. "I need a map of campus. A listing of the courses."

Sam didn't ask why.

He came around to her side of the booth and knelt at the end of it. He helped her lie down on the bench and pulled her legs straight, massaging her calves and thighs until they released from the position they'd held for hours.

"I'll help you up the stairs," he said. "Then I'll bring you some soup and a glass of wine. You'll need it."

Rose hobbled from the booth to the stairs, ignoring the people who came up, peered in the door, scowled at the Closed sign, and rattled the doorknob. She had work to do.

Her son's life... She had to imagine it so fully, so perfectly that he would once again be real to her.

She heard the voice inside, heard the questions, couldn't help it. Because she knew those questions were reasonable.

How do you know he lives in Vancouver?

Goes to university?

Takes English?

How do you know he's even…?

She never allowed herself to finish that question.

Rose hated the reasonable voice. This was not the time to be reasonable, this was the time to believe. So Rose imagined his life and ignored the voice.

She sat at the computer and brought all of her research skills to bear on the life of a twenty-four-year-old man in the city.

She researched nightclubs and coffee shops, boarding stores and army surplus. She surfed for music—concerts and CDs and indie labels. She Googled rental apartments and electric guitars and ski resorts. She looked into student passes for transit, the student union pub and the English Department's annual garden party.

She looked into spring-break trips to Whistler and Hawaii and Florida and California. She checked stats on male to female ratios on campus and even looked at online dating and even more quickly stopped.

Rose sat at the computer for hours, until her right wrist and arm and shoulder ached to match her tailbone and her head. She finished three bowls of soup, three cups of tea and one half of the bottle of red wine Sam had left with her, only knowing this because of the empty dishes sitting on the computer table. She certainly didn't remember eating or drinking, though, when she thought about it, she did feel better for it.

The sun had long since set, Sam snoring on the couch, when Rose gave up. She'd done her best for this day, done all she could to imagine him into being, but she knew it wasn't enough.

Because that tiny spark of doubt colored everything she'd done. No matter how much she learned, how many details of his life she included in her notebook, somewhere at the back of her mind lurked the opposite.

Her faith no longer absolute, Rose did what she could, knowing that it wasn't enough and not knowing what to do about it.

She turned off the computer, rubbing her aching eyes and pouring the last glass of wine from the bottle. She smiled at Sam, curled up on the too-short couch, and sat in the chair opposite him.

Maybe Sam would know what to do next. Or Mercedes. Or Doris. Or maybe even Rowena Dale.

Rose was surrounded by friends and family who always knew exactly what to do, but really, none of them could help her now. She needed to figure this out herself. She'd listen to their advice but she knew the person who counted, the person who could fix it, was her.

Oh, sure, Rowena's experience might help initially, but, in the end, the whole thing would come back to Rose, who would use what she could.

Over the years, Rowena had spent a lot of her millions checking out potential suitors. She was an expert on investigations and ways to get around the system. Rose made a note to call Rowena in the morning.

But none of this mattered, not really. Alive or not, her son was lost to her and Rose, finally, almost a quarter of a century later, needed to learn how to deal with that fact.

Sure, maybe Rowena's corps of investigators could find him but would Rose have the courage—or the right—to do anything about it?

No. It was his decision. She had wronged him, and he had the right to choose whether or not to see her. She'd made her choice a very long time ago.

With that decision made—Rose made another note to phone Mercedes in the morning and tell her not to call any investigators—she put down her notebook and touched Sam's shoulder.

"Time to go to bed, babe. You'll be all stiff in the morning if you keep sleeping here."

Sam opened his eyes and searched her face, looking, Rose knew, for her decision. When he found it, he nodded.

"It'll be fine," he whispered. "I promise."

And Rose believed him. Because she needed to. And because, sometime in the last few minutes, she might have found her son again.

CHAPTER 15

Doris felt lost. Richard was taking six months off and had taken over her position as head torturer.

He had arranged for the Way-Inn to deliver dinner on the nights no one felt like cooking and for the physiotherapist to come in every day.

Suddenly, Doris's reason for being was gone and she had no idea what to do with herself.

Caring for Emily, which had seemed so onerous at the beginning, now seemed like so little. And Richard, a man of charm and determination, had taken over much of her routine care. Which was, Doris reminded herself, the way it should be.

Doris missed Rose and Mercedes. She knew they were happier without the trek out to the house but she felt their loss. And she could not expect them—now that she had the time—to begin their morning sessions at the Way-Inn a month early. But she could—couldn't she?—go in to the Way-Inn each morning anyway.

Rose would be working, tourists would be in and out, a few regulars would drop in for coffee or an early lunch. She would not see Mercedes but at least one of the gossip queens—Doris herself—would be at her post.

As soon as she had that thought, Doris knew it was the right thing to do. She had always been uncomfortable about the summer hiatus, certain that there were things the gossip queens needed to know and do during those months.

She had, she realized, always resented the time it took them to get up to speed once September arrived. This year, Mrs. Doris Suzuki would ensure that no lag time intervened in the work of the gossip queens.

It was her duty to sit in their booth at the Way-Inn for two hours each morning. She would listen to stories, she would consider answers and, if necessary and Rose and Mercedes were unavailable, she would make decisions.

Doris felt a heady sense of freedom. And power. The gossip queens had always acted as a triumvirate, but she could, each summer for the foreseeable future, act on her own. She was capable of it and Rose and Mercedes would surely thank her for taking some of the burden from their shoulders.

A twinge of guilt touched her but she shrugged it off. She was doing the right thing. She knew she was.

Doris almost laughed out loud—something she seldom did—as she got into her car on Monday morning. Would it start? She had not driven it for weeks, had had no time or reason to leave home. *I have*, she thought, *been trapped here for months*.

She looked around at the neglected garden, the fading paint and unwashed windows. Doris's house, now the family home, had always been as tidy and perfectly groomed as had her own person.

She considered her spotted brown slacks and tan blouse, wrinkled and missing two buttons. Her shoes were scuffed and she had failed to put on either her watch or her earrings.

Doris angled the rearview mirror so she could see her face. No lipstick. Doris was not sure she had ever, even as a teenager, left the house without lipstick. And the raven's-wing black of her hair had overnight been laced with silver.

Doris bowed her head. Should she return to the house and begin again? No. Let the children have this time to themselves. She would stop at the mall and buy… What? Spray paint for her hair?

She pulled a pen and an old receipt from her purse—at least she had remembered her purse.

On the back of the receipt she wrote:

Lipstick.
Sandals.
Slacks.
Blouse.
Watch.
Earrings.

Doris could use these things again. It was not wasteful to buy a few new items for herself. And she could not represent the gossip queens looking like this. She slammed the car into Drive.

"And I need to do something about the house," she said, and quickly forgot about it as her trusty steed roared into action.

When Doris arrived at the Way-Inn an hour past her scheduled time of ten o'clock, it was definitely worth it. She was transformed. She wore white slacks, a black-and-white tunic and matching sandals. Her earrings and her lipstick were crimson, her watch silver. Doris smiled at the customers and at Rose as she marched to the booth at the back.

And then she stopped dead at the sight of a complete stranger sitting in *their* booth. She looked around the room—plenty of other places to sit—then back at the stranger. Pointedly.

She should have tried harder to convince Rose and Mercedes of the necessity for a sign. This would not have happened if they had followed her advice. She had even prepared a draft of the sign on sunshine-yellow poster board.

The Gossip Queens are in session.
Monday to Friday.
Ten to Noon.

Doris did not move from her stance in front of the booth. She was glad she had taken the time to go to the mall. She looked good standing there and the man in *her* booth would notice her. She would wait until he did.

She had learned even more patience over the past months since Tonika's accident and Emily's birth. Add that to the patience drilled into her as a child and Mrs. Doris Suzuki was prepared to stand by that booth for hours.

But Rose, sensing a potential disaster, hurried over with the stranger's bill.

"If you want to make the next ferry," she suggested, her back to Doris and her voice as sweet as chocolate syrup, "you should leave soon. Monday mornings are always busy."

Doris waited while he counted out the bills for Rose, adding what Doris considered to be a too-large tip before he slid out of the booth.

As he passed her, she looked up. He was very tall, slim and expensively dressed, a large gold watch adorning his wrist. She estimated his age—thirty-five to forty—and his income.

"Rose," she asked the moment the door closed behind him, "how long has he been here?"

"An hour? Long enough for two cups of coffee and breakfast. He read the *Financial Post* all the way through."

"I do not mean in the Way-Inn, Rose. I mean in Gibsons."

"I don't know."

"Of course you do. Sit," she ordered, sliding into the booth. "I need to ask you some questions."

Rose hesitated, looking around the café. But there was no one in the room except the two of them and so no excuse for Rose to avoid the interrogation. While Doris had been waiting for the stranger to move, the Way-Inn had emptied out, the tourists on their way to the ferry, the locals to work or Monday-morning errands.

"Let me get some tea," Rose said. "I'll be right back."

Rose does not look good, Doris thought. *She appears*

tired and sore. But as bad as she looked physically, Rose somehow looked better in herself, as if the weight she had been carrying all summer had lightened. Doris figured it was not gone, only lessened.

"That is two out of three," Doris said, as Rose sat down with the tray of tea.

Rose's eyebrows lifted.

"Huh?"

"Do not say that," Doris snapped. "'Pardon me' or 'excuse me' are more appropriate."

"Pardon me?" Rose repeated after Doris. "What in the hell are you talking about?"

"The three of us," she said. "You and I and Mercedes."

"Oh, I see. No, wait a minute. I still don't know what you're talking about."

She poured the tea, Earl Gray for herself, jasmine for Doris, who found herself missing Mercedes more than ever. She wanted there to be a third cup on the table, a third pair of hands, a third set of eyes.

She wanted Mercedes's help with Rose.

"I called her when I was waiting for the kettle to boil," Rose said, reading Doris's mind.

"Forget the two out of three. We do not have time for that now. I will tell you later. When will Mercedes be here?"

"Half an hour. She was finishing up the last room and had to have a shower."

"Good. That should be long enough."

"For what?"

"For you to answer my questions, of course."

Doris watched Rose. She might balk, but Doris thought not. Rose was the type of person who liked to please others and that was especially true with her friends. She also—like all of the gossip queens—had a healthy dose of curiosity in her makeup.

Rose might not be happy about having her questions placed on the back burner, but she was also stubborn and would make sure that Doris got back to where Rose wanted to go. It might take hours. Or days. Or even weeks. But Rose would not forget the two out of three.

"That man. Who was he?"

"He's from away," Rose said. "That's all I know."

Doris ignored the final statement. She knew Rose better than to give it any credence. Five minutes in Rose's presence and even the Academy Award auditors in their shiny black suits and ties would spill the beans.

Doris had never been quite certain what it was that Rose did to invite confidences from complete strangers. She thought it might be her sweet voice. Or maybe her ability to listen without even a hint of judgment on her face. Whatever it was, whatever Rose believed, Doris knew that Rose had much more information about the stranger than she admitted.

"Where did he stay?"

"Lord Jim's."

"How long has he been here?"

"Just since yesterday morning. He had to be in the office today."

"Has he been here before?"

"It sounded like it. He knew about the writers' festival and the craft fair and the dahlias."

He could have looked those up on the Internet, Doris thought. But he had to be the one. He was her only prospect.

So she continued to question Rose, making the questions smaller and smaller, pulling even the tiniest piece of information from her without remorse.

"His name?"

"Stanley."

"Stanley what?"

"I don't know."

Doris would call the receptionist at the resort. She had been at school with Tonika and would tell Doris his name, his marital status, and perhaps even which credit card he paid with. *Platinum*, Doris thought, *it would definitely be platinum*. She went on.

"A wedding ring?"

"No. No tan lines for a ring, either."

"He lives where?"

"In the city. On the water."

Doris increased her estimate of his net worth by twenty-five percent.

"What does he do for a living?"

"I don't know."

"Broker? Banker? CEO? Mining?"

Rose shook her head at each category. Doris knew that Rose knew this answer but she also realized that she would need to guess it correctly before Rose could confirm it. She tried again.

"Shipping? Real estate?"

Rose stopped her there.

"He's a developer."

And that stopped Doris in her tracks.

"A developer?"

"Yep."

"What is he doing here?"

"Duh, I don't know. Probably looking for some land to develop?"

Rose looked at her as if to say, "what else would he be doing here?"

Doris began to worry that her one prospect was gone, that a developer, someone who wanted to bring more people to live on the Sunshine Coast, someone who would chop down trees and put fences around beaches, someone who would destroy the habitat of birds and fish and small rodents, would never, no matter how handsome, rich or perfectly groomed, appeal to Mercedes Jones.

Still, she thought, *still.* Maybe his charms would outweigh his evil developer-ness. Maybe that perfect hair and teeth, those gorgeous lips and beautifully cut linen shirt had convinced Mercedes that her attitude toward that type of man needed to be reexamined.

Doris would know the minute Mercedes sat down across from her. She quit asking questions—they were going nowhere—and drank her tea.

She was seething inside. With questions for Mercedes, with plans to get the truth from her, with joy at being back where she belonged.

"I am not cut out to be a live-in, stay-at-home grandmother."

"No," Rose confirmed, pouring another cup of tea. "You're not."

"I will speak to Gray MacInnis this afternoon. I want to go back to work."

"But just for the afternoons," Mercedes interrupted as she slid into the booth next to Doris, pushing her into the corner.

"It's good for Gray and Josie to work together. And you don't need to work that hard."

"No," Doris repeated. "Just for the afternoons. One of us needs to be here in the mornings."

Rose and Mercedes looked across the table at each other and shrugged.

"Can't hurt," Mercedes said finally. "Septembers are always tough trying to get caught up."

"Okay," Rose said and sighed. "Maybe we're going to need that sign after all."

"And now," demanded Doris. "Tell me about Stanley."

CHAPTER 16

"I don't know anybody named Stanley. Oh, wait," I said, turning to Doris. "Maybe I do."

She looked at me suspiciously as if she knew that I knew what she wanted and hadn't decided whether or not to give it to her. She was already off balance because of our prompt acquiescence to her plan to sit in the gossip queens' booth. I was pretty sure she'd expected us to stop her from doing it by herself.

What she didn't know was that Rose and I had already talked to Richard about it, and had come up with a plan to give Doris a break by doing just what she'd offered to do. Win-win situation for us, though I was worried that we hadn't hesitated anywhere near long enough.

She was sure to be suspicious. I jumped back into the Stanley discussion even though I had no idea what it was about.

"Stanley," I said. "Right. He's one of the gardeners

at the dahlia place up the way. He retired about fifteen years ago, used to build bridges. Nice guy, and his wife makes those fabulous tourtières I buy every year at the craft fair."

I turned to Rose, a cat's grin on my face.

"That's next weekend, isn't it? I can hardly wait. I need to buy some mugs to match those gorgeous plates I got last year."

I tried not to think of Mr. X, talking of the mugs, but of course I couldn't stop myself. And I could see Doris's eyes narrow in concentration. She could read my mind, I knew it. And then, to make it even worse, because I was there in front of Doris, I did something I hardly ever did. I blushed.

I watched her face for clues. Had she seen the blush? If she had, Stanley the gardener would be her prime suspect. I concentrated on blushing even more obviously but felt the color fading from my cheeks. Damn.

I laughed at myself. There were days, months, maybe even years—and this was shaping up to be the worst of them—when I was all kinds of an idiot.

I grinned at Rose and waited to see if she would pick up the ball I'd thrown.

I didn't often get a chance to tease Doris and at the

same time save my own ass. I planned to drag this out as long as possible.

Rose played along. She grinned, nodded at me and said, "I want to buy one of those wooden pieces—the five-foot-high playing cards. I hope I get there early enough to get the Queen of Hearts."

Doris looked ready to stomp her foot through the floor. "Not *that* Stanley. Someone from away."

"Well, Stanley is from away. Or at least he used to be. Oh, yeah, there's tour-bus Stanley, too. He's from away."

Rose piped up.

"He's a nice guy except for his teeth."

"I just try and ignore them," I said. "But—" I turned to Doris "—they are the worst false teeth I've ever seen."

"But they're not as bad as his toupee." Rose giggled. "I don't know how he does it with the false teeth and the toupee, but he always has some gray-haired momma on his arm when they stop in on their way back to the city."

Rose turned to Doris and I caught a glimpse of her evil grin as she did so. I sat back and prepared to enjoy myself.

"Doris," she said, her voice so sweet and calm, "maybe you can tell us—" she nodded to include me in the *us* "—what we're missing when we look at tour-bus Stanley. I think he's a nice guy but he's stuck in the seventies. Bad teeth, worse toupee, and those baby-blue leisure suits. Yet every trip all summer he toddles off at the end with a different woman on his arm.

"What is it," she asked, and I watched her pause to carefully pick her words, "what is it that women of your age—smart, well-dressed and attractive women—see in tour-bus Stanley? What am I missing?"

She sat back and so did I, waiting for the blast. It didn't happen.

"Many women," Doris said, her face serious, "of my age, and even of yours—" she looked pointedly at me "—are lonely. There are few men of our age and tour-bus Stanley is a nice man. He still has a job and beneath that leisure suit, along with a still-beating heart, is a reasonably attractive body."

"Oh," I said, "you're right."

I was surprised, but when I thought about the thin, tanned man who occasionally brought one of his women to the Sand Dollar, my surprise diminished. I'd learned to put the couple in the suite farthest from my door.

Neither Stanley nor his women had lost anything in the way of lung capacity, that was for sure.

Doris was taking Rose's questioning seriously and hadn't caught on. I knew that because she tried again.

"Not *that* Stanley, either." She tried to keep her voice low and restrained, but it kept rising out of control. "Someone new this summer," she insisted.

I looked at Rose, who shrugged and mouthed, "I don't get it."

I did. I didn't know where Doris had gotten the name *Stanley* but I sure hoped that wasn't Mr. X's name. Tour-bus Stanley had given me an aversion to that name.

"Sorry, Doris. I don't know any other Stanleys."

"What about that developer from the city who has been staying up at Lord Jim's?"

I looked a question at Rose.

"He was in for coffee this morning on his way to the ferry."

"Oh."

I wasn't sure where to go with this. I wanted, desperately, to ask questions.

What did he look like?

How long had he been here?

When was he coming back?

Was he married?

How old was he?

But if I asked a single one of them, Doris would figure everything out. She couldn't know if he was Mr. X, but her suspicions about the man she thought I was seeing would be confirmed. She would never stop until she found out who he was, why I didn't know anything about him—including his face and his name. She'd figure out where I'd been seeing him and then…

Who was I kidding? She wouldn't stop even if I didn't ask a single question. In fact, she'd probably be even more curious.

I needed to hit the exact right balance. A couple of questions, not too personal. I needed to hold her off until tomorrow. Because if he showed at the beach and Stanley wasn't meant to be back, it couldn't be him. And I needed to know at least that much even if I wasn't quite ready to turn around and see his face.

So I asked them as nonchalantly as possible, hoping against hope that Doris didn't discern my concern.

"A developer?" I asked. "Is he looking at those beach acres up around Sechelt?"

There, I thought, that's perfect. Nice detail about the beach.

Doris looked disappointed. It had worked.

"We do not know," she said, glaring at Rose, "what property he looks at, but I will find out."

Although that statement sounded like a threat, I knew better. It was a promise. No one was better than Doris at finding out information and, once I thought about it, assuming Stanley wasn't Mr. X, her search into the developer's life would keep her busy long enough for me to decide what to do.

"That's a good idea." And I left it at that.

Rose didn't get the hint.

"He's very good-looking." She smiled, her eyes dreamy and glazed. "Not at all my type, too polished for me, but—" she looked over at me "—definitely Mercedes's."

Damn again. No. Only damn if Stanley *was* Mr. X and I was pretty sure he couldn't be. Checking would be good.

"Has he been around for a while?" I asked, carefully keeping the eagerness from my voice.

"This is the first time I'd seen him. And I'd remember his face," Rose said. "And his accent."

"His accent? What accent?"

Oops. An error in judgment. Okay, a *serious* error in opening my idiot mouth before thinking.

Doris's eyes glared at me like a hawk on a bunny. I'd given away oh, just about everything, I moaned to myself, with those four stupid words.

Rose, oblivious to the important game going on beneath the surface, answered my question.

"He's got a lovely English accent. Kind of like Pierce Brosnan as James Bond. Sort of looks like him, too."

The good news, if there was a single speck of it from this fiasco of a meeting, was that none of the Stanleys—not gardener Stanley, not tour-bus Stanley (thank God) and not developer Stanley—were Mr. X. He sounded just like anyone on the west coast of North America. Only better. Not different. Just better.

I waited to see what Doris would do. She had three options as I saw it.

She could ignore the fact he hadn't been here before yesterday—and it was a fact, *everyone* stopped in at the Way-Inn and Rose *never* forgot a face—and continue pursuing information about developer Stanley. That was the best option for me.

She could abandon Stanley and begin the search, more seriously now she had confirmation that her suspicions were accurate. Still not too bad for me. No one had seen us together and, whoever Mr. X was, if his identity wasn't obvious to me it wouldn't be to Doris, either.

She could begin her interrogation right now. This was the worst option for me as Doris was, this morning, back to her old self. She would drag the details from me within half an hour.

Her thought processes shone on her face. I watched as she rejected option one. She hesitated over option two and moved on to option three. I saw the exact moment she decided against it, breathed a sigh of relief before I began to wonder if she'd thought of a fourth option I hadn't, then relaxed as she chose option two.

I wondered why she had, but not too hard. I was too relieved to be overly curious.

"We will have to keep an eye on this Stanley character," she finally said. "We do not want the wrong man—even if he does look and sound like James Bond—developing our beach."

As I walked back to the Sand Dollar all of the stuffing fell right out of me. I felt like the scarecrow from *The Wizard of Oz*. My legs were wobbly and the straw from my neck and head seemed to be tugged out of me by the wind. I felt light-headed and practically legless.

Relief had never before hit me so hard. Not when Julie and Ron finally found each other; not when Sam's cancer scare had turned out not to be; not when the bank approved the mortgage on the Sand Dollar. Not even when I found out that the bastard who'd fathered Julie had died in a car accident up coast. He'd never again hit another woman.

I realized that the strength of my relief was in direct proportion to the strength of my obsession. And that scared me. Because I still lacked the courage—or at least I had this morning and for the fourteen mornings before this one—to turn around and see his face.

And if I couldn't face him, how was I to deal with this obsession? How was I to get my life back to normal? I couldn't deal with this much longer.

Tomorrow, I thought, I'll do it tomorrow.

And then I prayed for rain.

CHAPTER 17

Rose wasn't sure exactly what had happened between Doris and Mercedes that morning, but there had been something going on.

She wasn't a part of the secret and she didn't care. She was having enough trouble keeping her own end up, keeping careful track of every thought, even those thoughts buried so deep she needed a backhoe to bring them up to the light of day.

She relegated all despairing or unhappy thoughts to the dungeon, slammed the door on them and threw away the key. The only way to keep her son safe was to know that he *was* safe. Rose refused to shirk that duty, even though at times—oftentimes—it felt impossible.

Sam seemed satisfied with her change of mood. He disregarded the plates she broke every day, just placed an order with their supplier for new ones.

"This happens every summer. We lose more plates in these two months than we do in the other ten."

And that was true, though Rose was pretty sure they'd never had a summer quite like this one.

Sam also ignored the several times a day he had to scurry to redo an order botched by Rose's inability to remember the difference between tuna salad and shepherd's pie. Or coffee and beer.

The bruises were, as she told him and he chose to believe, simply a natural result of perimenopause. Kind of like PMS, she said, only longer-lasting.

Rose had never appreciated Sam's inability to see that she had any flaws as much as she did now. His refusal to get angry or even cranky about her mistakes, her anxiety, her restlessness, was the thing that made daily life possible.

And his willingness to play the imagination game—to help her imagine the boy into being—was what made it bearable.

Having Doris in the Way-Inn every morning would help. Not having to listen to Tonika's pain—Rose had never admitted to anyone, not even herself until it was over, how deeply those sounds had affected her—helped even more. Now, if she could just get Mercedes over every day....

She would work on that. An offer of dinner might work. Mercedes hated the kitchen and only needed the slightest of excuses to abandon her tuna salad or peanut butter and banana sandwiches.

Rose still wasn't sure how Julie had grown up to become so beautiful living on Mercedes's diet. Or why Mercedes herself, for that matter, was so attractive. Mother and daughter had skin to die for—clear and flushed with color. Hair shiny as a just-groomed red setter and strong white teeth.

She tried to hate them for that. One potato chip and Rose's skin grew a zit to match. And chocolate? One bite, one zit. But of course Sam didn't care, so Rose treated herself once in a while.

But what she really envied was their disregard for every single eating rule. The Canada Food Guide? What was that? Five helpings of fruit and vegetables a day? They were lucky to get five a week—if you didn't count the bananas which went with the peanut butter. Rose wasn't sure Mercedes even knew what a salad was.

But Rose knew that what she really needed was something over which she had no control.

She needed her son. She needed him to contact the adoption agency and say, "I want to find my birth mother." And to live close enough to the Sunshine Coast that they could accomplish that meeting right away. Then she needed to see him. And she needed him, most of all, not to hate her.

That wasn't too much to ask, she thought in her few reasonable moments. It really wasn't.

The rest of the time she knew that she'd never see him, that she didn't deserve to, and that she shouldn't push her luck. She'd made a better than good life for herself.

She had the perfect man, a job she loved and the two best friends any woman could ask for. She had a whole peninsula full of friends and neighbors, all of whom loved her.

Rose's life couldn't be better.

Now if she could just convince herself of that.

But, she thought, as she rushed through the maze of tables of the Way-Inn—tour-bus Stanley and his latest flame were ensconced in a back booth, grinning and playing footsie under the table—no matter how hard she tried, she couldn't do it. She couldn't forget that one little flaw in her otherwise perfect life.

The one good thing that had come out of the last couple of days—besides Doris taking up her place in the gossip queen booth—was that she knew therapy wouldn't help. That was also the bad thing. Because it meant that she wouldn't be getting better in September when she had time to go to the city.

It meant that this bruised, light-headed, forgetful, scared side of her was as good as it was going to get.

Rose sighed and headed back to tour-bus Stanley's booth with a Pimm's for the lady (no surprise—her Englishness was obvious a mile away), and a gin and tonic for Stanley. Since he usually drank rye and ginger, Rose figured it was a ploy to help win the lady's heart. Or whatever. But based on the evidence in the booth, the ploy was unnecessary.

The sight of tour-bus Stanley reinforced Rose's decision to call Mercedes about dinner. Yes, their conversations would be rushed—dinnertime was always frantic—but she thought it was Mercedes's presence, her funny and wise and calm presence, that she needed, not the talk.

But she did want to ask Mercedes about Doris and what exactly had been going on this morning. What was all that about Stanley? And Mercedes's blushing? That might just have been a first.

And Rose, although she didn't know it at the time, then followed exactly in Doris's footsteps, which wouldn't have been a surprise to either of them. Or to Mercedes.

If Rose concentrated on the mystery of Mercedes,

Doris and Stanley, she would be able to distract herself from her own messy life.

Mercedes hesitated no more than a nanosecond before saying, "Yes."

Of course, Rose phrased her request to Mercedes carefully, but she probably hadn't needed to.

"Mercedes? I don't think I'm going to make it to September without some help."

"I'll be right there."

"It's not that urgent. Really. Doris being here in the mornings will help but the evenings are the worst. Would you do me a favor?"

"Of course."

"Will you have dinner at the Way-Inn for the next few weeks? On us, of course."

"I'll pay for my own dinner."

And it was solved. Rose would have Mercedes's comforting presence each evening and she'd be able to figure out the whole Stanley thing.

Doris hadn't phoned, so whatever she was thinking or researching wasn't yet complete. If there was one thing Rose knew about Doris it was that she wasn't a big fan of the whole delayed-gratification thing. When it came to gossip, Doris was of the spill-the-beans-right-now school and it didn't matter if it was the middle of the night or pre-dawn gray. Doris would pick up the phone whenever the gossip struck her.

Rose felt better, not good yet, but better. Sam, Doris and Mercedes would be her anchors.

"Three better be enough," she muttered, picking up the barely touched drinks and extravagant tip from tour-bus Stanley's table.

She thought about phoning Mercedes to warn her that he was on his way to the Sand Dollar but figured Mercedes had seen enough of Stanley's habits to be expecting him.

"Anchors aweigh," she said, racing into the kitchen and dropping the glasses on the counter. Only one broke.

"I'll get it," Sam said, pushing her away from the shards of glass. "You'll cut yourself."

Rose thought she heard another word—"again"—but she had to be wrong. If Sam had said it, he too was beginning to crack. Because that word, in that context, in that tone of voice, was as close as Sam had got in the past twenty years to getting angry or impatient with Rose.

"I'll be careful," she whispered as he passed her with the broom in hand. "I promise."

"It's okay, babe. I just don't want you to hurt

yourself. And," he said, swatting her on the butt with the straw end of the broom, "I want you to find me indispensable."

Rose leaned into him.

"You don't have to clean up after me to do that. I couldn't live without you."

She kissed his neck right below his ear, where she knew it would make him shiver, flicking her tongue out to taste his skin. His body curved toward her and then straightened.

Rose used his favorite line, "Remember where we were," and kissed him again. "It's getting busy out there. I've gotta go."

Rose felt his parting smile and its promise as a physical presence while she served friends and strangers alike. It helped slow her down, getting through a whole hour without breaking a thing or collecting a single bruise. She did drop a few knives and forks and one mug, but it didn't break so she didn't count it.

Mercedes arrived just as the first rush was over.

"I'll sit at the counter. We'll be able to chat."

Rose knew she meant to chat about Rose's problem, but Rose had a different plan in mind.

"What's the whole thing about Stanley?"

She had turned away to pour a glass of wine for Mercedes but turned back just in time to catch the blush. She almost dropped the glass.

"Mercedes? Don't tell me. You and Stanley the developer? Where'd you meet him?"

"It's not Stanley at all. At least I don't think so. Or at least not that Stanley. Or maybe it is. Or not. It might be Stanley."

"Stanley the developer? It *can't* be tour-bus Stanley."

Rose pushed aside the flicker of doubt she'd felt saying it, keeping her fingers crossed. "It can't be."

"It's not tour-bus Stanley or gardener Stanley. And I'm pretty sure it's not the developer."

"Pretty sure?"

Rose refilled Mercedes's glass and poured one for herself. She could see she was going to need it. She plunked the half-full bottle on the counter and herself on the stool next to Mercedes.

"Huh?" she said, the question as coherent as she was capable of being at this time in this particular conversation.

Mercedes said nothing, simply drank her wine and looked at the menu until Rose ripped it from her hand.

"If you haven't memorized this menu after twenty years, I'm sorely disappointed."

Mercedes looked away from Rose and shrugged. Mercedes sheepish? Yet another first.

"This Stanley thing is really bugging you, isn't it? You're definitely not yourself."

Rose ticked off the clues on her fingers, gaining momentum as she went along.

"One. You blushed when Doris got too close this morning. And you *never* blush.

"Two. You didn't answer me when I asked.

"Three. You blushed again this evening.

"And four. Now you're looking sheepish.

"Come on, Mercedes, give. You made me talk the other day. It can't be as serious as that."

Rose took a long look at Mercedes and saw doubt on her face and a little touch of panic in her eyes.

"Mercedes? Stanley the developer? Is he your son?"

Finally, a response from the real Mercedes. She laughed so explosively the wine in her mouth ended up all over the counter. Rose automatically wiped it up with the cloth in her hand, patting Mercedes on the back until she could breathe again.

"No child," she sputtered, "except Julie, I mean. I think this is where it all started. With Julie and Ron."

"Huh?" Rose said again, lost somewhere at the beginning of the story. "Stanley knows Julie and Ron?"

She brightened as she figured it out. Or thought she had.

"He's Ron's dad? You're right, that is a bit awkward."

"Ron's dad isn't in the picture. At least not in my picture. And forget Stanley. He's Doris's construct. I'm pretty sure he's not called Stanley." She seemed to think for a minute. "Although I suppose he might be."

Rose poured herself more wine and waved the bottle at Mercedes. "You?"

"Yes."

"Okay," Rose said, a few minutes of wine-sipping under her belt, but still feeling confused. "Maybe you can tell me. I'll try and put Stanley out of my mind." She paused. "Although I have to say that developer Stanley is a fine figure of a man. And rich, too."

"I'm sure he is," Mercedes replied. "But he's not Mr. X."

Rose didn't bother to repeat 'Mr. X' although it took severe restraint on her part not to. She hoped the look on her face would work, because she felt like a parrot following along behind Mercedes, repeating her every word like a fool.

"So? Who is he?"

"I don't know."

That time Rose had to clap her hands over her mouth to stop from repeating those words. "Oh," was the only word which seemed safe. And then she got it. Or she thought she got it.

"You met him online."

Rose was proud of herself. Doris loved the computer with a passion but she hadn't figured this one out.

Mercedes laughed again.

"I wish."

Rose was getting mad.

"Mercedes Jones. That's enough. I'm not going to keep guessing. Either you tell me the story or you don't. What's it to be?"

Mercedes shrugged.

"I'm not ready to tell it yet."

"When will you be?"

"Tomorrow. I'll tell you—and Doris—at dinner tomorrow night." She seemed to think for a moment. "At least I hope I will."

Rose smiled a wicked smile and patted Mercedes on the shoulder.

"We'll have dinner at six. I'll call Doris."

Mercedes nodded.

"There's one thing I have to do before then but

it's not totally dependent on me. I may not be able to…"

"Oh," Rose said with confidence, "oh, you will tell the story tomorrow night. We'll make sure of it."

CHAPTER 18

Doris felt better than she had in all of the months since Emily was born. The head torturer's job had passed from her, she was able to enjoy Emily as a grandmother rather than with a mother's responsibility, and most of all, she was finally getting out of the house.

She had not realized, in the years since Mr. Suzuki had died, in the years since she had gone to work at the *Sunshine Coast News*, how much her life had changed.

For the first five decades of her life, Doris had followed—with the appropriate patience and grace and dignity—her allotted path in life.

She had cared for her parents and her grandparents. She had married a man of whom they approved. She had borne a lovely child and cared for her, her husband and her home. And then everything changed.

Her daughter, trained by Doris to live as she had—with patience, grace and dignity—had married an appropriate man and moved to an appropriate home of her own. Shortly after that, Mr. Suzuki, seemingly healthy and strong, had gone in for a checkup to find that his good health was an illusion. Within months he was gone.

Tonika had convinced Richard to sell their new home and move in with Doris so they might look after her. But that was not what happened; Doris had spent all her life looking after others and she could not now break the habit.

Tonika lived with it for a year and then had a conversation with her mother, a conversation which Doris could not, in either a million years or her wildest dreams, have anticipated.

"Mother," Tonika began, handing Doris a cup of tea, "I need to look after my husband. It is my purpose, that's what you taught me. I should also be looking after you. That's right as well."

Doris was unsure of how to respond to this. It was true that she occasionally felt some bitterness. It was true she had anticipated a certain amount of freedom once Tonika had married.

She had not anticipated her husband's too-early death. Nor Tonika's insistence on moving home nor Richard's acquiescence to her insistence.

Doris had not understood how deeply ingrained her

caring had gone. She had told herself, when Tonika and Richard moved in with her, that it was now their home. She had transferred the house into their names, but she could see now that it had not been enough.

They had lives that needed to be lived. They had to have a chance to be adults, to be the caregivers for each other. Doris saw the necessity of that.

"Yes," she said to her daughter. "All you have said is true."

She looked into the face of her daughter and smiled.

"You are very wise," she said. "Wiser even than I. I will move into an apartment so that you may…"

Tonika stopped her with an impatient "No, that's not at all what I'm saying. You need a life, Mom,"reverting in her impatience to the less formal address.

"I, we, want you to stay with us. But I thought—" She paused and Doris wondered what would come next. She braced herself.

"I thought you might want to try getting a part-time job."

Doris felt something crack in her heart. She thought that it might have been the chains of duty she had worn for so long because what she felt after the crack was freedom.

She smiled and saw the shock on her daughter's face.

"Daughter, you are a most amazing person. That is exactly what I should do, exactly what I want to do."

In the end, what began as a part-time job answering the telephone for Gray MacInnis became a full-time vocation. After an entire lifetime, Doris knew she had found who she was meant to be and what she was meant to be doing.

And now she could see that she had not been cut out to be a mother or a nurse to either her sick husband or her injured daughter, and this despite the fact that it was precisely what she had been taught as a child to be.

It had taken her own child to see Doris's potential and to help her fulfill it. And that was why Doris had happily given up the life she loved to care for Tonika and Emily.

She thanked all the gods she could think of that she had been pushed back out into the world and the life she had finally learned to live.

"Gray," she said, walking into the offices of the *Sunshine Coast News* that afternoon. "Josie."

She and Josie had met many times since Josie's arrival and her usurpation of Doris's job. Doris had long since conquered her anger at Josie. The two of them—Gray and Josie—were good together and Doris was proud of her part in their meeting.

"I would like to come back to work," she told them,

glancing pointedly at the piles of paper fluttering in the breeze from the open windows. "But only for the afternoons. The gossip queens have decided to work throughout the summer and I am the one who is to stay in the booth in the mornings."

Gray grinned at her and stepped forward to take her hands. He lifted them to his lips and rained kisses on them while Josie giggled.

"Doris, you are a lifesaver. I don't think I could have made it through another whole summer without knowing what was going on."

He kept kissing her hands while he talked, and when Doris tried to tug them away, he just held them tighter.

"You are a goddess, an angel, a miracle worker."

Doris could not help herself. She pulled one hand loose and patted his head.

"I worship at your dainty little feet."

Kiss.

Doris was glad she had been shopping and was wearing her new sandals. She tried to stop the giggles, tried to keep her mouth firmly shut, tried to think of something sad, but the continuing kisses tickled her into giggling. Once started, she did not want to stop.

Kiss. Giggle.

Giggle. Kiss.

"Okay, you two," Josie said through her giggles. "Mrs. Suzuki..."

"Please," Doris managed. "Call me Doris. I am no longer so formal with my friends."

"Doris, then. When did you want to come back to work?"

"Tomorrow?"

Josie and Gray nodded in complete agreement.

"We're so busy," Gray said. "If you hadn't walked in, I had an ad laid out for the paper for tomorrow."

Doris's disbelief must have shown on her face, for he tugged at the hand he still held and guided her to his computer.

"See? There it is."

Gray grinned over her head at Josie; she could feel the grin zinging across the room.

"I'll print it out for you."

Doris waited until she was back in her car before she reread the words she'd seen on the screen.

> We know we can't replace Doris Suzuki—she's irreplaceable—but the *Sunshine Coast News* is looking for a smart, funny, compassionate, organized person to work afternoons until Doris is ready to

come back to us. Don't worry. We won't compare you to Doris Suzuki. No one could pass that test.

If someone had tried to place that ad during Doris's tenure at the paper, she would have been appalled at their lack of professionalism and would have tried to discourage them from using it.

Now? Now Doris planned to stop at the dollar store and pick up a frame for the table beside her bed. She wanted to see those words every morning for the rest of her life.

CHAPTER 19

I couldn't sleep that night. I'd promised to tell Rose and thus, at the very least, Doris, if not the whole rest of the world. I hoped that the gossip queens would decide, as they had with Julie and Ron, that this story held a conflict of interest great enough that they couldn't spread it.

Rose, okay. Doris, if necessary. And it would be. But the whole of the Sunshine Coast? No way. At least not until I knew who he was. Right now my life felt complicated enough without adding a horde of friends and acquaintances dropping in at the Sand Dollar ostensibly to *see* how I was doing.

Somewhere around two o'clock I came to the conclusion that it was a good idea—if the conflict rules held—for Doris to know the story. Once she knew and was bound to secrecy, she wouldn't be out stirring up everyone's curiosity by asking questions about me.

I'd have to remember to drop in to the Way-Inn in the

morning and invite her and Rose to dinner. At my place. I didn't want to make a fool of myself more than once. Or in a public place. And Rose could bring the food.

Once that was resolved, I went on to fretting about the real question. And it wasn't how much to tell Rose and Doris. Once I decided to tell them, my only option was to tell the whole story.

No, the question was far more complicated than that. And it came in multiple parts.

Was he going to be on the beach in the morning?

If not, the story would end without resolution.

If he was—and this was the kicker—would I turn around?

I spent the rest of the hours of darkness fretting about it.

One minute I was absolutely certain that I would turn around. The next there was no way, not even if hell (or the Sunshine Coast) really did freeze over. In August.

My head ached and my stomach churned. And the clock on my bedside table clicked inexorably closer to dawn.

When I finally dragged myself out of bed and into the shower, I was no closer to an answer. In fact, the two options buzzed through my head like a horde of raging wasps.

And I swear my head hurt just as much as it had when I had been stupid enough to walk onto the porch of the Sand Dollar without checking for nests.

This was to be my big investment. Doris and Rose's, too. I'd be able to move out of the tiny apartment Julie and I rented and make a better life for both of us.

The Sand Dollar had been abandoned by the children of the last owner almost ten years earlier, but I thought I could turn it around. What it needed, I was certain, was love, elbow grease and time, and I had plenty of all of them.

It was September. If I did this, I needed to have it up and running by May. Most of my income for the year would come in that five-month period from May to September.

I had signed all the papers and the Sand Dollar was mine. And Rose's. And Doris's. And the bank's. Mostly the bank's, although there was a little bit owing to the shady finance company down the road.

But I was full of enthusiasm. Julie was at Doris's and I, in my boots and overalls and toolbelt, was all set to get started. The office and apartment first. And quickly. I'd already given our notice and we had to be out of the apartment in five days. I couldn't afford to carry the mortgages and pay rent as well.

I could make this place at least habitable in five days. I could.

It didn't work out quite as planned. I stomped up onto the porch, my boots ringing on the steps, put my key in the handle and threw open the door, upsetting a wasp's nest right above it.

Upset wasps don't give a damn whether you actually meant to disturb them. They're worse than a bunch of curlers watching the final end of the Tournament of Hearts.

No excuse is enough, no apology sufficient.

The wasps seemed particularly angry about my hair.

After I'd run down to the water and straight in, screaming at the top of my lungs all the way down the rickety dock—I'd have to fix that as well—after I'd cooled off enough to assess the situation, I ended up with ten stings and ten painful, itchy lumps on my scalp.

I was lucky. Any more and I'd probably have ended up in the hospital. This way I was only a day behind while the exterminator got rid of the half a dozen nests he found hanging from various parts of *my* motel.

So was I or wasn't I going to turn around?

I was halfway down the beach and I still didn't know the answer to that question. I'd reversed direction at least ten times and then forced myself around and headed back down the beach.

I must have looked like a complete idiot. Travel north. Stomp, stomp, stomp. Stop. Whirl around. Travel south. Stomp, stomp, stomp. Stop. Whirl around. Travel north.

I wanted to see him. I didn't want to see him.

If it weren't for Rose and Doris, I'd leave it to him to make the first move. I felt safer not knowing who he was.

There was no possible way Mr. X could be suitable. I knew I'd had that same conversation with myself at least a few times since the first day, but there were no suitable men on the Sunshine Coast.

No matter how many times I had the conversation, I came up with the same answer. No suitable men on the Sunshine Coast. And that meant when I did find out who he was, I would also discover just why he wasn't suitable.

I wanted to leave things the way they were.

I liked the anticipation I felt walking down the beach each morning, the way each step felt like a step into an unknown and exciting future. I loved the way the sand felt under my feet and the air caressed my skin.

I felt conscious of the world and its effect on me in a way I hadn't for a very long time. My body reacted to everything, every sound, every touch, every smell and taste, instead of just ignoring them and moving on.

And I especially enjoyed the waiting once I sat down on the rocks and focused my gaze on the water.

My heart beat faster. Not unbearably so, just enough to make me conscious of its beating. My skin tingled as if I'd come in out of a storm—each pore scoured by the wind and rain and changed by the experience.

My hearing became acute. Each sound—from the gentle ruff-ruff of the waves to the calls of the seabirds as they started their day—fell on my ears with precision. But even though I concentrated, I had never yet heard him arrive behind me.

And unlike in horror films, I never jumped or screamed when I heard his voice over my shoulder, hadn't even the first time.

I loved that time on the beach—it made me feel alive and excited and aware, and I didn't want to spoil it. But I no longer had the option of allowing it to develop on its own time.

I sat down on the rock with my thermos and I waited. This day, the perfect August morning, was wasted on me. I was tired, my head and eyes and stomach ached, and even the French roast in the thermos wasn't helping.

My head drooped and I spun off into sleep. I couldn't help myself. The sun warmed my head and I drifted away. I woke to the feeling that I'd just missed something incredibly important, something which promised to change my life.

He was no longer on the beach but he'd been there. My thermos was empty, his cup carefully placed next to it, both of them out of the way of my arms and legs in case I woke up flailing.

My temple glowed with memory and I knew he'd kissed me before he left. I knew he'd sat at my back for at least an hour, his warmth and closeness allowing me to sleep.

And I knew who he had to be even before I opened the note he'd left tucked underneath the thermos. And I didn't know why I hadn't thought of it earlier.

I'd never heard his voice but I should have recognized those beautiful hands. I'd noticed them before—many times over the years—and I couldn't believe I hadn't made the connection.

Because there was no one else it could be, no one else on the Sunshine Coast who it could be.

The note, written in an almost unreadably messy hand, said only:

I've finished your coffee. Thank you again. I'll see you tomorrow. Joseph.

Joseph. The hermit who lived in a cabin down the beach. The man whose secret was so sad no one ever dared ask him about it. The hermit who played chess and listened to Bach on his wind-up record player. The man whose past was so dark that once a month he sat in the Way-Inn and drowned his sorrows, sitting silently, drinking until his head sank onto his shoulders and he could forget the thing that had brought him here.

No one knew what it was except maybe Rose. And maybe Gray MacInnis who, despite being the owner and editor of the *Sunshine Coast News*, held closely many of the secrets of the peninsula.

I didn't know his last name. Probably no one did. Joseph was a quiet man. He'd said more to me in the past few weeks than anyone had heard him speak in ten years.

I took that as a good sign, because everything else had to be bad. Not because of who he was, but because once I'd put a face and body to the hands and voice, the hook, previously only caught in my cheek, was now securely and permanently settled. I could neither shake nor pull it loose.

I had believed that the lust and longing I'd felt over

the summer wasn't really about me, but about something outside of myself. *I don't really want a man*, I thought, *I want the idea of a man*. My envy of Julie's relationship with Ron wasn't about her, not really, but about the image of that relationship.

Knowing who Joseph was changed all that. Because now it really was about me. It was about a man, a very particular man. One with problems—oh my God, he had problems—but with an appeal I couldn't deny.

And the thing that worried me the most? Once I figured out who he was, I realized that I'd often thought of him, watched him in the Way-Inn, walked by his cabin on the off chance I might see him.

My longing hadn't been undirected at all. It had been directed toward a specific person. And now what in the hell was I going to do? I settled for picturing him.

Tall and thin, his face scoured clean by years of pain and the ocean wind. He was my age, more or less, but his face appeared ageless.

I wondered why I'd never consciously noticed before how beautiful he was, how he moved, how his body seemed the most comfortable part of him, as if that was where he lived.

But I knew that couldn't be true, wasn't possible for the part of his life before he arrived on the Sunshine

Coast. Although he lived in a cabin on the beach, Joseph was no ordinary hermit—if there were such a person.

I was both happy and sad that I knew who he was. Knowing meant I couldn't tell Rose and Doris. Knowing meant my longing—and my lust—had blossomed into something almost uncontrollable. I wanted to see him, to touch his face, to take that kiss on the temple about a thousand steps further. And more than anything else, I wanted to see if the pain in his eyes disappeared when he looked back at me.

This fragile whatever—I couldn't call it a relationship or even a friendship—we had begun was too delicate to share, too easily damaged.

And that wasn't because he was a hermit. People on the Sunshine Coast looked after their own and Joseph was one of us. No, I worried that even the hint of a story would send both of us scurrying back into our caves, never to meet again.

Because to Doris, to Rose and especially to me, he was perfectly and absolutely suitable. In fact, I was surprised none of us, even in jest, had thought about it before.

"Respect," I said, walking back up the beach. "That much pain? We wouldn't push him. He'd have to come out of it on his own."

Even though he'd taken what I chose to consider as

the first tiny step, almost anything might push him back. Certainly it would take time and patience.

And that was true for me as well.

I thought about Julie and the way she rehabilitated abandoned dogs and cats. She sat patiently, not making eye contact but there, just there, her sweet presence filling the space with warmth until the animal couldn't resist reaching for it.

That's what Joseph and I had been doing for weeks. He'd been doing it for me, and I for him. Now he'd taken it one step further. What would happen next? I didn't know.

But how, I wondered, was I going to let this thing develop at its own pace and still keep Rose and Doris happy enough to stop searching for Mr. X? I had, I looked at my watch, exactly nine hours to figure that out.

The good news was that most of those hours would be spent cleaning the rooms, including my own. I definitely had to pick up the glass, the drywall dust, and hide the holes in the wall. Housework was the best possible occupation for thinking.

Hands busy, mind occupied just enough to stop me from getting bored, and plenty of time to try out a dozen stories.

And I picked up the glass and the drywall dust and

hid the holes in my wall even though Rose had called me halfway through the work to say we'd meet at the Way-Inn. More room, she said, and she needed to keep an eye on the new waitress.

By the end of the day I still didn't have a story. Not one that would work, anyway. I tried out way more than a dozen, maybe as many as a hundred.

I tried variations on the "he's from away" theme. I thought up a whole series of "I can't tell you, he's married…famous…rich" plots. I even, in desperation, considered quite seriously—if only for twenty seconds—using tour-bus Stanley.

It was five o'clock and finally, in the shower, I thought of it.

The most obvious story and the most likely to succeed. It was the "I met him on the Internet" idea. I came up with dozens of those stories, all of which seemed pretty darn reasonable to me. I polished the best one until it shone like the sky on the morning after a storm.

I met him on the movie blog I'd just recently become addicted to. That would work because of my new satellite dish. He lived in… I wavered between Dallas and Miami but finally settled on Miami. It wasn't easy to get here from there.

His name was Al. He was from Cuba, he worked as

a firefighter and he designed and installed very upscale kitchens on his days off.

No, I didn't have a photograph but he was divorced, had two children—a boy and a girl—and five grandchildren.

He loved movies and we'd been e-mailing back and forth for a few weeks. I didn't know if we'd ever meet—the conversation hadn't gone that far—but it was nice to have someone to talk to when I couldn't sleep.

There. I brushed off my hands. That should work. It answered many questions and contained all kinds of good reasons why the others couldn't be answered.

"I am the mistress of the art of misdirection," I yelled at my vacuum cleaner. "I am the goddess of storytellers."

The afternoon raced by into evening as I added more and more details, trying not to think about the morning and Joseph.

Rose and Doris had a kind of seventh or eighth sense about matters of the heart, and if I told the Al story thinking of Joseph, they'd pick up on the disconnect.

It wasn't easy, but I was sure I'd managed to push Joseph from my thoughts until I hit the front door of the Way-Inn.

What if he was inside? What would I do? What would *he* do?

"Wait, Mercedes Jones. Just hang on. He never comes to the Way-Inn in the summer. Never."

I'd reassured myself, but by then it was too late. I wasn't going to pull off the Al story because Joseph was in my head. All the work I'd done since five o'clock, all the hours I'd spent polishing the Al story and ignoring Joseph were wasted.

And I had absolutely no idea what I was going to do now.

Rose and Doris were waiting in the back booth, their faces bright with anticipation. Me? I was totally unprepared. I felt like a teenager walking into a math exam when I'd spent the night cramming for history.

Damn. And double damn.

"Well," Doris said, pouring me a glass of wine. "Time to tell the story."

CHAPTER 20

Rose wasn't sure she wanted to hear Mercedes's story. And she wasn't sure Doris did, either, despite her demand.

She looked at Mercedes, her head down and hands wrapped around her wineglass. She didn't look any too keen to jump into the storytelling.

What was up with the three of them? She knew the reason for her reluctance and Doris's was probably the same. They both needed the distraction of looking for whatever or whomever Mercedes was trying to hide.

But Mercedes? Last night she'd seemed okay about it. Tonight she looked as if telling them the story might be the last thing on earth she wanted to do. What had happened between last night and this one?

Rose would find that out eventually. In the meantime, she was going to make sure Mercedes didn't ruin her plans for the next few weeks.

"Mercedes. Honey. You okay?"

"I'm fine."

She looked up from her contemplation of the tabletop and smiled. Not her regular I'm-so-happy-to-see-you-two smile but a smile that appeared to have been glued on with not very effective stickum, a smile that kept fading on and off.

Doris must have caught it, too, because she said, "You do not have to tell us, you know. The story, the telling of it, can wait until you are ready."

"What if I'm never ready?"

"That is also fine."

And that, Rose knew, was a lie. Doris never let a story go. She was willing to step back and let it ripen a little, but let it go? Never.

But Rose nodded anyway, feeling more than slightly guilty. Which was kind of weird because what Rose wanted was also what Mercedes wanted. At least it looked that way. But she still felt guilty.

"We're your friends. You tell us what you want, when you want to."

She felt better having said that, but the improvement didn't last long.

"Yeah, but you're also gossip queens. I don't tell you, you'll start looking."

Mercedes glared first at Doris, then at Rose.

"You will, won't you?"

Rose was certain her expression matched the sheepish one on Doris's face.

"Of course you will." Mercedes sighed and returned to contemplating the table.

The resignation in Mercedes's voice was clear and Rose couldn't leave it like that.

"If you don't want us to look, just say so."

Doris said, "We will not do anything you do not wish us to."

"Don't look, okay?" Mercedes said, her voice subdued. "It would only make a complicated situation impossible."

Rose wondered if Doris had jumped to the same conclusion as she had. Mercedes must be seeing someone completely unsuitable. Probably married. Maybe too young.

And it had to be someone from the Sunshine Coast or she wouldn't care.

Rose ran through the possibilities in her mind and then slapped herself down. No, she thought, don't go there. Don't even think about who it might be.

She looked at Doris. The two of them were definitely going to require a support group to get through this—both of them had natural instincts that compelled them to chase a story like a cat in a room full of catnip.

"I don't know, Mercedes," she said. "I don't know if I can stop trying to figure out who he is. Not look for him? Probably. But not think about him, not look at the possibilities? Impossible."

Mercedes shrugged. Doris smiled.

"I am with Rose on this, Mercedes. You wish us not to look for this man and we will not do so. But we would be lying to you if we said that we will not wonder about it."

"Maybe that's all I can expect," Mercedes said. "Thanks for that much."

Rose solved her own dilemma and assuaged her guilt by changing the subject, by saying something she never thought she'd say out loud.

"I think I'm going crazy. I've spent the last week imagining exactly what my son is doing."

"That's natural," Mercedes said, throwing her a look of gratitude.

"Of course you think of him," Doris said. "Any mother would."

"No, it's not like that. I mean, I even know what books he carries in his backpack and I don't even know for sure if he's going to school." She paused and then said it, the thing she'd been avoiding for years until Mercedes had made her admit it, the real reason she and Sam didn't have children of their own. She cleared her throat, clasped her hands on the table, and said it.

"I don't even know if he's still alive."

Doris and Mercedes reached out to touch her hands. Rose pulled them away.

"He could have died in a car accident. Or drowned as a baby. He could be in a coma somewhere right now. Or what if he had leukemia? Or ran out into the street chasing a ball? Or a dog?

"No," she said. "Don't touch me. Don't. There are a million things that might have happened to him." Her voice grew shrill, spiralling up to the ceiling.

Rose took a breath, spoke more slowly. She didn't want Sam to hear her losing it now he thought she was getting better. *She'd* thought she was getting better. But saying it out loud?

That was the one thing she'd sworn never to do and here she'd done it twice.

Rose thought back to the day she'd made the promise. She was fifteen, shaking with pain and fear and sorrow. The four-bed hospital room was empty except for her.

The nurse had said, "Don't worry, sweetie, we'll put you in a room of your own so you don't hear the babies." She'd even brought Rose some flowers—pink carnations—which looked a little worn, but cut through the smells of the hospital with their spiciness.

The delivery had been difficult. She'd been warned about that—too young, undeveloped, too tiny—but Rose had ignored the warning and the suggestion that she go to prenatal classes.

Now, three days later, she was getting ready to go home. In a taxi because her dad couldn't get the time off work and because he couldn't bear the thought of his little girl in pain.

She sat on the bed, the blankets wrapped around her. She hadn't felt warm in months. Rose knew her boy was gone, home with his parents, the only parents he'd ever know, and she missed him already.

The same nurse who'd brought her the flowers had appeared in her room that morning, a tiny bundle in her arms.

"I believe babies, all babies, do better with a blessing from their birth mama," she said. "Your boy's on his way to a new life but somewhere in his heart he'll always remember you.

"I'll be back in five minutes." She placed the baby into Rose's waiting arms. "You tell him what he needs to hear."

And Rose didn't even ask what that was. She knew. And she told him.

"I love you, baby, more than anything. And I know you'll have a wonderful life."

She worried about the tears falling onto his sleeping face but he just opened his eyes for a moment, yawned and went back to sleeping.

"Here's the thing," Rose said. "Here's the only thing I can do for you.

"I promise that I will never forget you, that I will always think of you, always watch other boys as you grow up so I know what you're doing, so I can see you as you grow."

She kissed his salty forehead.

"I will believe in you," she whispered. "Always."

Rose kept her promise for almost twenty-five years, never once allowing herself to think of him as being anything but healthy and happy.

She knew his life as well as she knew her own. The neighborhood he grew up in, the friends he played with, his first bike. She knew the day he went to school and how easy it had been for him to learn to read, as if he'd just been waiting for someone to open the door when he hadn't quite been able to reach the handle himself.

She knew the day he first kissed a girl—he was eight—and when he first kissed a girl in earnest. She knew when he broke his arm snowboarding and his ankle playing football.

Rose knew he liked chocolate chip cookies and salt and vinegar potato chips. He read voraciously, everything from Harry Potter to Homer. He loved NASCAR, hockey and the Cameroonian Lions playing soccer.

He was a brat and a practical joker. Boys and girls liked him and quite a few girls fancied themselves in love with him. He hadn't yet reciprocated, but he was thinking it might happen pretty soon.

And through all those twenty-odd years, Rose had never once admitted it, even to herself, never once said, even in the darkest hours of the night, that she was scared to death.

Because she believed if she didn't say it, it couldn't happen.

She'd said it twice that week and was trying desperately not to think about what that might mean. But she saw it in the faces of her friends, and in Sam's face when he thought she wasn't looking. They thought exactly what she tried so hard not to—her son might be dead, might have been dead for a very long time.

Or even worse, his death might have triggered her anxiety, her mother's instinct somehow knowing he was gone.

Rose had an idea that the second thing was the true thing. And she had, just this moment, thought of a way to check.

She didn't remember the exact day her anxiety had begun but she knew it was somewhere around the beginning of summer.

Doris waited to interrupt her, taking the solemn breath and making that slight gesture, palms up and out, that meant she had something to say.

Doris would change the subject trying to get Rose, as she often did with both Rose and Mercedes, to put her saddest thoughts away. When a problem couldn't be solved, when sadness threatened to overwhelm them, Doris changed the subject.

And Rose laughed to herself. She had just done the same thing for Mercedes, who had let her do it.

And so did Rose. She let Doris change the subject and she smiled at Mercedes to reassure her. "It's good," she mouthed. "I need a break."

"I am going back to work at the paper starting tomorrow. They need me and, more importantly, I need them."

Rose checked to see if the shock she felt was reflected on Mercedes's face. It was.

"*You* need them?" Mercedes asked. "*You?* Mrs. Doris

Suzuki, the queen of standing alone, is admitting right out loud before everyone—" Mercedes flung out her arms to encompass the entire Way-Inn "—that you need someone? Wow. I'm impressed."

"Me, too," Rose chimed in, trying to suppress the idea that had bubbled up the moment Doris announced her intentions, trying to concentrate, for a moment at least, on Doris instead of herself.

"This calls for another bottle of wine."

"Yes," Doris said, "I know it is unusual for me to admit this, but I have learned a great deal in the past six months."

"Tell us," Rose suggested. "Maybe it'll help me."

"Me, too. I definitely need some wisdom. Speak, oh wise one." Mercedes laughed, raising her glass in salute. "Tell us what you have learned."

"And it had better be good," Rose muttered. "Because wisdom is definitely eluding me this summer."

Doris raised her glass in return and said, "It will not take long because these are lessons both of you learned a very long time ago. It is just that they were so foreign to the way I grew up it took me a long time to learn them.

"I learned that love and openness are more important than anything when raising children."

"I don't know about that. Look at all the trouble I had with Julie, and you couldn't have raised a child with less discipline and more love than her."

"Mercedes, your Julie is a perfect child, as is Tonika. But in Tonika's case, I am certain that she became that way more in spite of me than because of me."

Rose and Mercedes both grunted in disagreement but waited for the second lesson before they really jumped in.

"I learned, just yesterday, that I was not cut out to be a wife and mother but to be the woman I have become in my old age."

Rose couldn't let that go. "You're wrong, you know. I think we all change and the person you were at thirty might not even like the person you become at sixty. Change is good. Change is inevitable."

Mercedes laughed and poured more wine.

"Doris, I don't think I ever told you this before and I should have. You're my role model—you and Rowena Dale. Twenty years from now, I want to be just like you."

Rose nodded and watched while Doris, normally so undemonstrative, first blushed and then let a few delicate tears roll slowly down her cheeks. She didn't even try to mop them up.

"Women get to have more than one life, and just

because you love your new life doesn't change how good the first one was."

Rose was very proud of herself for that statement; it was perfect. And had the added benefit of being true.

"Actually, the first one was not good at all. I only survived it because of Tonika and the discipline I learned as a child. Mr. Suzuki—" she paused, and Rose saw her decide quite deliberately to continue "—was not a good man."

Rose didn't know what to say or to do. Her image of Doris changed with those few words. The woman she'd known—graceful and living a perfect life—became a different woman. Rose couldn't help but wonder whether that would some day be true of her as well.

But of course it wouldn't, because now her friends knew her secret, her deepest fear.

And as she thought that, she reached for Doris.

"I know how hard it must have been for you. To live with a bad man."

"An evil man," Doris interrupted, her hands resting still as death in Rose's.

"An evil man. But you're here, Tonika and Emily and Richard are here. And you have a new life."

Mercedes added her hands to the pile.

"Okay, enough grizzling. We need to keep drinking

because I, for one, couldn't bear to hear one more secret today. It's enough. Let's put them aside for tonight and deal with them..."

"Along with our hangovers." Rose giggled.

"Tomorrow."

That night, for the first time in his career at the Way-Inn, Sam was the one who had to call the sergeant to pick up Doris and Mercedes and take them home. He escorted them to the car, placed his hands on their heads as he'd seen on TV, and helped them into the backseat.

"Go slow," he said, poking his head into Ron's window. "I don't think bumps or quick turns are a good idea."

And then he carried Rose home, her body light and warm in his arms. He made her take some aspirin and drink some water and then he placed her on the bed, lay down next to her, a smile lighting his face when she began, ever so delicately, to snore.

CHAPTER 21

Tonika woke Doris at noon.

"If you're going to work today, you'd better get up."

She handed Doris a cup of coffee and some aspirin. "Here, take these. You look terrible."

Doris, her head threatening to split into a dozen little pieces and her stomach ready to exit through her throat, took a few minutes to understand. Not Tonika's statement, but her presence in Doris's room.

She leaned against the dresser, crutches under her arms, fully dressed and ready for the day.

"I am seeing things," Doris said, brushing her hands over her eyes to clear them. "Ghosts. Hallucinations."

Tonika laughed and Doris's heart wanted to break in two at the sound. She had often wondered, over the hell of the last few months, whether she would ever hear Tonika's laugh again and here it was. Her heart skipped another beat.

"Should you be up?"

"Of course, and so should you. You don't want to be late on your first day back."

Tonika turned, teetering a little on her crutches, her teeth clenched and her jaw tense with pain. Doris knew better than to offer to help, and besides, she was absolutely certain that if she hurried out of bed, one of two things would happen. She would throw up or her head would explode.

By the time the coffee was finished and the aspirin had begun its job, Doris felt almost well enough to get up. She remained unsure about the shower or the sunlight so she took a bath instead and put on her sunglasses.

She had forgotten that she had been driven home by the sergeant until she opened the front door and found Richard waiting to drive her down to Gibsons.

"Your car is at the paper," he said. "But if you don't feel up to driving, I'll come down and pick you up. Just call me."

Doris would have laughed at the carefully noncommittal tone of voice and expression on Richard's face but the laughter would hurt too much.

She understood now how Mr. Suzuki had felt all those years, why he insisted on complete silence in the mornings, why he worked the afternoon shift even though his seniority would have allowed him to switch to days.

She understood why he was always so withdrawn and why his temper overwhelmed him so much of the time. She understood his need for solitude and his discomfort with Tonika.

What she did not understand, what she would never understand, is why he did not give it up. How could he bear to feel this way every single day? This was Doris's first hangover and she would make certain that it was her last.

But Mr. Suzuki had felt this way every single morning of his adult life. Maybe he felt even worse, Doris thought and, for the first time since she had discovered his secret, she felt a pang of pity for him and the terrible life he had lived.

She would waste no time thinking about what *she* might have done differently, but one day she would talk to Tonika about her father. Because Doris knew now that he deserved their sympathy, even if not their love.

Any one who felt this way day after day must have continued because he had no choice. Mr. Suzuki's drinking, his solitariness, his bad temper, were a way, Doris supposed, to drown his black hole.

She understood that need. She, too, had found a way to do the same thing. Her discipline, learned as a young child, was used as a teenager and an adult to hide from herself.

"If I am seen as perfect," she had thought at the time, "no one will be able to tell how scared I am, how flawed I feel. Least of all myself."

Mr. Suzuki had simply chosen a different path to the same place. Doris put this insight away to deal with at another time. Right now she needed to get through her first day back at work without revealing the shakes, nausea and headache she carried with her.

At the paper, Josie greeted her with a hug and another cup of coffee.

"I'll put the bread in the toaster," she said. "A slice of lightly buttered toast will help."

Doris groaned and once Josie had disappeared into the back, she dropped into her chair. Her desk looked just as it had when she left a lifetime ago. So much had happened, yet here she was and everything seemed to be back to its pre-accident self.

The only thing changed was Doris. The only thing new was the way she saw the world.

It did not embarrass her, as it would have even two weeks ago, that Josie knew what had happened last night.

And besides, she might as well get used to the notoriety. If Josie knew, everyone on the Sunshine

Coast knew as well, even if all three gossip queens had been out of commission. Maybe *especially* because they had.

The new Mrs. …no, wait, she thought, I will drop the *Mrs*. The new Doris Suzuki will not be ashamed of showing her emotions, both good and bad. She will tell people how she feels. And she will start right now.

When Josie returned with the coffee and toast, Doris took a careful bite and a slightly less careful sip.

"Ouch," she said, though the new Doris Suzuki had, for a moment, considered the use of *damn* instead but had decided that it would be better not to go too far at the start.

"Thank you, Josie. This is very considerate of you."

"Oh, Mrs. Suzuki…"

Doris held up one hand to silence her. "Please, call me Doris."

"Doris. I've been there. I don't know why you needed to go home via Rose's special transportation, but I understand."

"Yes, and so does almost everyone else on the peninsula. But I thank you anyway. I would not have thought of toast but it has made my stomach feel better."

"In a couple of hours you should eat some protein. Drink as much water as you can and I promise you that you'll feel much better tomorrow. Think of it as a twenty-four-hour flu."

Doris smiled and settled into her space. For the next four hours she had no time to worry about how she felt. Every phone call was for her. Every person who walked through the door came to her desk. Some brought flowers, others just a 'welcome back.'

People asked about Tonika and Emily but their first words were always for Doris.

"I'm so glad you're back. I missed you," Rowena Dale said. She shot a glance across the room to where Josie sat engrossed in her computer. "I like her a lot but she's too young to really get it."

"How are you, Mrs. Suzuki?" the Scoutmaster asked. "The boys have been asking about you."

"We've missed you."

"We're glad you're back."

"This place wasn't the same without you."

Each time someone spoke a variation on the final sentence, Doris looked up at Josie, who invariably grinned back at her and said without rancor, "No, it wasn't, was it?"

And when Doris told them she'd be at the Way-Inn each morning in the gossip queens' booth, their already-big smiles threatened to split their faces.

"Every morning?"

"Monday to Friday except holidays. There are too many tourists on the weekends and holidays."

"Starting now?"

"Yes, starting tomorrow and right through the rest of the summer."

Doris had decided to do this for her own benefit, but it seemed everyone was delighted she would be there.

By the end of the day, her cheeks hurt from smiling so much and her desk was full of gifts.

Doris knew she had made the right decision once she had driven slowly and carefully home. Tonika sat in the rocking chair with Emily sleeping on her lap and Richard next to her, holding a glass of wine for his wife.

"Dinner's almost ready," Richard said in a whisper. "We're just waiting for Emily to wake up from her nap."

The tears fell from Doris's eyes onto Tonika's hair, but this time all of them knew that they were tears of joy.

"You look so perfect together."

She kissed the top of Emily's head and then repeated the gesture with Tonika.

"I love you, all of you."

She reached over to Richard, kissed the top of his head, and then hurried to the door.

"I will finish dinner," she said over her shoulder. "You stay here. Together."

When she had left the paper this afternoon, Doris had believed that her life was as good as it could possibly be. She had been wrong. Seeing Tonika with Emily and Richard had made everything indescribably better. Doris had not made a mistake by going back to work.

She was not deserting her daughter and her grandchild. She would be a grandmother, not a surrogate mother. That would be the right role for her.

She explained this to Rose the next morning, with tears and laughter in the appropriate places. Rose, as always the perfect audience, smiled and laughed and shared in Doris's tears of joy.

And then she said, "I'm glad you went back to work, Doris. I need your help."

"What?" Doris asked. "Anything you need. Of course."

"I need you to check the obituaries. I need to know if my boy is dead."

"There are thousands of obituaries every week. How can we do this?"

Doris did not want to discourage Rose, but it was an impossible task. Twenty-four years' worth of deaths, even if they only looked in the city, might take months to sift through. Without a name, without a location? Rose's son would never be found.

"Rose." Doris patted her hand. "We could search for months and even if we did not find him, we could not be sure. He might have moved out of the province, even out of the country. His death might not have been reported. If he lived in a small town, the paper might not be online. This is an impossible task."

Rose did not look as sad as Doris had expected her to appear at this statement. She did not look sad—or even worried—at all.

"It won't be as hard as you think. I know his birth-date. I know he lives in Vancouver."

Doris did not believe that Rose had any way of knowing that he lived in Vancouver but she nodded her acceptance anyway.

"This narrows it slightly but it is still not enough. Twenty-four years will take a long time to search and, in the end, we will still have hundreds, if not thousands of names. Many children—babies, toddlers, school-children—die each year. And many young men as well.

"Once we get the names—which will take a long time—we will have no way of knowing if one of those names belongs to your son."

Doris did not want to hurt Rose in this way, but she

did want to stop her from chasing an impossible dream. This quest could only come to a very bad end.

But Rose still did not look the least bit discouraged.

"Do you know his name?" Doris asked.

"No."

"Then how…"

"I know when he must have died. If he did," she added, and now the sadness Doris had been waiting to see finally appeared.

"I've spent his whole life believing that he was okay, living a fine and happy life with his mom and dad. I didn't ever doubt that.

"I promised him that my belief in him would never waver, that he could count on me to keep him safe. I knew in my heart that my promise would do just that.

"But a few months ago I started to worry about him, wondering if he was ill, or injured. He can't have died before that," Rose whispered. "He can't."

Doris wished for Mercedes. But she was at the Sand Dollar and so Doris tried to think of what Mercedes would do.

She slid out of her side of the booth and around to where Rose sat. She put her arms around Rose and hugged her as tightly as she could, whispering in her ear like she had learned to do with Emily.

"It will be okay, Rose. Everything will be fine. You are going to be okay and we will find him, I promise. Everything will be okay."

She rocked Rose and whispered over and over that everything would be okay, although Doris was now quite sure that it would not be.

She believed in intuition. Too many times she had anticipated an injury or some sorrow, too many times she had been right. Rose's concern had to mean something.

"Rose," Doris said, putting her hand on Rose's downcast chin and tilting it up so their eyes met. "You are right to think that something has changed.

"Look at me," she insisted. "But I do not think that it inevitably means that your son is no longer with us."

"What else could it mean?"

"Many things. He may have moved away, out of reach of whatever link you have forged between you. He may have fallen in love, or out of it, for the first time. Think about Sam. If he is paying attention, you know where he is or what he is about to say—just like you do with Mercedes. And sometimes with me. But if we are focused completely on something else—as I have been with Tonika and Emily—do you still feel that connection?"

Doris watched while Rose thought, her brows lowered and the lines between them sharp and straight.

"No, you're right. I thought I'd lost all of you—Mercedes and you and Sam—along with him. I even thought I'd lost my ability to read customers."

"That might have been partly because you were so focused on him, but Mercedes and I have been locked into our own journeys these past few months."

Doris realized that she, too, had seldom been able to hear her friends over the past months. She had not known who was telephoning before she picked up the receiver, had not known when Rose or Mercedes needed to hear from her.

That had changed sometime during the past couple of days and Doris was grateful for it. She was old enough to begin worrying about losing pieces of her mind, even those as unreliable as intuition. She was glad it had returned.

"So he might still be all right?" Rose asked, her expression slightly less fraught with the fear she had been wearing on it for weeks.

"I think it is possible," Doris said. "If you are certain he lives in Vancouver…"

"I am."

"And you give me the date you began to be anxious about him, then I think I can check tomorrow and may be able to tell you right away. Because you have a date and a birth date, I will check everywhere in Canada. We can begin with that."

"I need to do something and this feels like something." Rose smiled and patted Doris's hand. "You were right about the gossip queens. We need you here, even during the summer."

CHAPTER 22

I sat on the dock, a bottle of wine in the cooler beside my chair, and tried to decide what to do. Not just about Joseph—though that was the biggest part of it—but about Rose and Doris, too.

They wanted to know who he was, how we'd met (not that we really had met), what would happen next. I could tell them his name, but I couldn't tell them who he was.

Because I didn't know.

I wasn't sure anyone did.

He was the hermit, the tall tanned man who lived in a tiny cottage on the beach, who spent one night a month in the Way-Inn, spoke to no one and invariably got taken home by the sergeant.

I knew that because I'd seen him, but Rose had never told me anything about him, although I was sure she knew something. But she never spoke of what ailed the people she sent home with Ron and, somehow, I knew enough to resist the impulse to ask.

Just as I knew she wouldn't tell anyone Doris's reasons or my reasons for being offered a lift with Ron, she wouldn't tell me Joseph's reasons. Not once, in all the years she'd arranged those rides had I heard even a glimmer of gossip.

People might say, "So-and-so got a ride with the sergeant last night," but they'd say nothing further. They wouldn't speculate about the reasons, at least not out loud.

Everyone on the Sunshine Coast seemed to understand that there were times—maybe for every one of us—when the world grew to be too much, when whatever pain we felt threatened to overwhelm us. And because we believed that we, too, might be sitting in Ron's squad car one day, we were careful to keep any unkind thoughts we might have about the riders to ourselves.

Joseph, Josie Harris, me, Doris. Many others. It seemed to be about a deep-down aching pain that couldn't be dealt with, could only be drowned. And that only temporarily.

So what pain did Rose see in Joseph? I didn't know. And maybe even he didn't know.

Joseph played chess with Fred. I knew that because I'd found Fred there one day, and because Fred mentioned him once in a while. But Fred never said more than, "I'm going down to play chess with Joseph."

No one talked about Joseph. His life, like Ron and Julie's love, was too important for gossip, too painful for discussion. All of us understood that.

People left Joseph food and clothing—carefully choosing a time when he was asleep or out so as not to embarrass him with their generosity. Joseph, in return, never spoke of these gifts.

I knew he neither needed nor used them. And I only knew that because last winter during the tourist lull I helped Julie at the animal shelter thrift shop one day a week.

Late one rainy and dark November night, someone knocked on the back door. Before I could fight my way through the hanging clothes, the piled-up furniture, the books and records and toys, he was gone, two bags left behind on the stoop.

I knew it was Joseph because I caught a glimpse of him under the streetlight.

I recognized the clothes in the bag because Rowena Dale had bought them for one of her fiancés and they were brand-new when she stormed up to the Sand Dollar, bags in hand and as furious as a half-drowned cat.

"What am I going to do with these now?" she yelled,

pulling wool slacks, silk shirts and linen jackets from the bags and throwing them on the floor.

She stomped and ripped at them, unsuccessfully, until I stopped her.

"I'm going to drop them off with Joseph," she said. "He can use them. Better him," she added, calming down enough to pick up the clothes and stuff them back into their bags. "Better him than that man who made a fool of me."

Two days later, those clothes sat on the back stoop of the thrift store. Julie told me later that Joseph was her most reliable donater. He regularly left bags of clothes at her door.

As for the food people left? I didn't know for certain, but once I knew that he didn't keep the clothes, I suspected Joseph took those bags and dropped them at the food bank.

He was older than me, but not by much. I knew that not by his face but by the way he moved. When I saw him on the beach or on the street into town, he moved quickly and without aches and pains, despite living in an unheated cabin practically in the ocean at high tide.

The things I knew about him—except for the clothes and food—were things that everyone in Gibsons knew.

The things I knew about him that only I knew were few. I knew he liked French roast coffee and that he had mugs that matched my plates. He supported, fed and clothed himself.

I knew he walked the beach in the early morning.

He knew who I was, knew my name. And I knew I'd never forget the way it sounded when he spoke it.

I knew he had the messiest handwriting I'd ever seen and I wondered, just for a moment, whether he'd once been a doctor. Or a piano player.

Because I also knew he had the most beautiful hands I'd ever seen. And his body ran hot, I could feel his heat even when he wasn't touching me.

That was all I knew.

People gossiped here like they did everywhere, but there were things—true love, great despair—that were too deep, too serious to be talked about. Joseph was one of those things.

But these past weeks, it seemed to me that the man who had joined me on the beach, who said my name in *that* voice, who sat behind me and kept me warm while I slept—that man had worked his way out of despair.

I couldn't know whether that was true, not for sure, until I'd seen his face.

Joseph seldom left the beach or, if he did, I seldom

saw him. I knew he had to go into town to buy groceries, but I didn't remember seeing him in the stores. And especially not during the summer.

It was as if he, like all the tourists who came to the Sunshine Coast, took a trip away from the place where he lived the rest of the year. And I wondered where he went or if he stayed on the beach but was careful not to be seen.

If that was true, I couldn't blame him. There were tourists who would insist on taking his photograph—like they took mine—to show their friends back home.

"This is the hermit who lives on the beach," they'd say to their friends. "He's not very friendly, though. Or maybe he can't speak."

I didn't blame Joseph for avoiding that particular summer treat.

If he had gone away over the past summers, he hadn't done so for this one. But I hadn't seen him anywhere but the beach, hadn't heard of his regular monthly visit to the Way-Inn or if he'd dropped into the thrift store.

Maybe, I thought, maybe I was the only one who knew he was around. Maybe I was the only who'd seen him. And why would that be?

The wine was gone and so was the last faint hint of

color on the water. I watched it fade until only the shine of the water separated it from the night.

Stars appeared, their reflections sparkling both up and down. The moon lit the night, drowning the stars in the water with her light, until only she could be seen below.

I stood and stretched, listening to the sounds of laughter somewhere down the beach. Somehow I'd lost my laughter this summer, but I could feel it, curled deep in my belly, waiting, stretching itself just as I had. It showed up occasionally, with Doris and Rose, but it was waiting.

Well, I wasn't waiting any more.

It was time for action.

I didn't sleep much that night, but I had no trouble getting out of bed in the morning. My pre-dawn walk down the beach seemed full of portents. Birds flew in the dark, songbirds sang their desperate songs as I passed, the waves spoke to me with each step.

The first rays of sun hit the beach as I reached the rocks and clambered out onto them, thermos and blanket in hand. The blanket was wishful thinking. Perhaps, I'd imagined during my sleepless night, we'd talk for hours and we'd be thankful for the padding.

My body had gone much further than that, imagining a naked tryst on the morning beach.

The laughter uncoiled itself at that thought. By eight o'clock the beach would be full of curious tourists. No tryst. But I carried the blanket with me, anyway.

I announced my intentions by sitting facing the beach rather than the water, not north, not towards his cabin, but inward. I wouldn't see him until he reached the rocks, but once there, I would be facing him.

I sat, trying not to fidget, a cup of coffee steaming in my hands, my eyes closed and my breathing deep.

"Focus," I whispered to the water, "on the waves. Think of water, its colors, its life. Not of him."

And for a few short moments, I succeeded.

A shadow covered the sun and a sudden chill touched my body.

"Mercedes."

I saw only shadow, the sun limning his body with light, black center shading to azure edges.

"Coffee," he said, a hand moving out of shadow to appear before me. "Please," he said. "I didn't sleep very well last night."

"Neither did I."

And then I was lost. My carefully prepared plan flew out to sea, my mind following right behind.

"May I sit?" he asked, indicating the rock next to me.

I nodded, unable to speak. I wasn't ready to see his

face. Yes, I'd seen him, in the Way-Inn in the dark, on the street. But I'd not noticed his face, not really.

What if? There were a million of them zinging around in my mind like pinballs bouncing off bumpers. Lights flashed. Bells rang.

What if?

He just wanted to be friends.

He was lonely, just wanted someone to talk to.

He was married.

I looked away as he settled onto the rock beside me, his warmth dispelling the what-ifs.

Turning, I faced him for the first time.

"Joseph Kennaday," he said, holding out his hand.

"Mercedes Jones." Taking his warm hand into mine.

"I know."

"How?"

"I've seen you at the Way-Inn. On the beach. Around."

"How do you know my name?"

"This is the Sunshine Coast. Everyone knows you. You own the Sand Dollar. Your daughter is marrying Ron in September. You're one of the gossip queens."

He laughed, a wild, booming, irresistible laugh and my laughter rose up to join it.

"It's not as bad as it sounds," I finally said.

"I'm sure," he said, nodding his head formally, "I'm sure it can't be as bad as it sounds."

"We do good work," I said, hating the defensiveness in my voice. "Help people, make sure…"

He held up his hand. The sunlight shimmered off the waves, throwing shards of light back into the sky.

"It's fine, Mercedes. Whoever you are, whatever you do. It's fine."

His hand moved, slowly, allowing me time to decide, as I'd allowed him. His fingers gently touched my cheek, moved across my face. They moved from my cheek to my temples, across my eyelids, as if learning my face via Braille.

His eyes opened when he reached my mouth, his fingertips soft and slow-moving, sweet and salty as I touched my tongue to them.

He blinked, his breathing quickening to match mine.

And then he backed away, his eyes as fearful as mine felt.

"I'm not ready," he said.

"Neither am I," I admitted.

But what I wanted to say is that no one is ever ready for love. It's like taking that year off or having a child. You just have to do it, because if you wait for the right time, you'll never do it.

I wanted to tell Joseph that we were old enough to take the risk that it wouldn't work, to jump right into the fire that flamed between us.

But I didn't have to.

"I don't want to wait," he said, his fingers soft on my cheek. "But there are a lot of things you don't know about me. The main one is that before I moved out here, I lost my wife and children in an accident. I blamed myself and, until this summer, I wasn't sure I could get over it. I won't forget them, not ever, but I'm ready to move on, to get on with the things I need to do."

I wanted to ask him about his family, about what those things were. I wanted to beg him to tell me now. I absolutely didn't want to think about Rose and Doris waiting for the story.

"I'll wait. Not forever," I said, "but it's summer. It's a good time to have something to look forward to."

He smiled and nodded. "Thanks," he said. "It won't take long."

Joseph leaned toward me and kissed my eyelids. When I opened them, he was at the end of the spit. As always, I hadn't heard him move.

"Tomorrow?" he asked.

"Of course," I answered. "I'll bring the coffee."

CHAPTER 23

Rose lay in bed and watched the ceiling, waiting, as she had for most of the summer, for it to crack over her head. This night, though, she thought when it cracked it might reveal the night sky. It might crack open just like one of those baseball domes where the roof peels back and the sky appears.

Rose wasn't sure what had changed for her. She still wasn't sleeping; in fact, she had been awake all night and the pale-gray light of dawn had just arrived at her window. Yet, here she was, imagining the night sky through her cracked ceiling instead of a crushing fall of plaster enveloping her.

By the end of the day, she thought, *I'll know. And I won't have to pretend anymore.*

She couldn't wait any longer, not even for Sam's sake. She knew getting up would wake him. She knew he needed his sleep. But she couldn't wait.

The weight of the ceiling above her, the light touch of the sheet on her body, Sam's breathing next to her. They all oppressed her. She needed out.

She left a note on her pillow.

> I've gone to the Sand Dollar. I want to walk on the beach and Mercedes is sure to be up. I'll see you later.
>
> Love, Rose.

The *love* was salted with tears.

There would be an ending in this day.

Rose walked up the hill to the Sand Dollar, arriving just as the sun peeked over the mountains behind her.

"Mercedes?"

She cupped her hands and peered into the front window. No movement. She hammered on the door. She rang the doorbell. No response.

Rose hurried to the back and the bedroom window.

"Mercedes?"

She was starting to panic. Where could Mercedes be? And then Rose figured it out. She smiled and then grimaced.

She'd figured it out and she couldn't tell anyone, not

Doris, not even Mercedes. She'd promised. But she grinned again.

Mercedes was meeting someone on the beach in the mornings.

"I can't believe I didn't figure this out before," she said to the bedroom window. "All the clues were there. I'd phone first thing in the morning and Mercedes would be out. She didn't come to the Way-Inn for breakfast more than once or twice all summer."

Rose laughed to herself. All the information had been there, just waiting for her to wake up and put it together.

"What do I do now?"

The bedroom window didn't answer.

"I can't tell Doris."

The window listened obligingly. Rose took that as a *yes*.

"But she deserves to know. Or she'll keep looking."

The curtains stirred in the light breeze and Rose waited for another sign. There wasn't one.

"I want to tell her."

Of course you do, the breeze whispered in the trees. *You want to be the one to tell her. You want to be the winner.*

"You're right. And that's not fair to Mercedes. That's just me being selfish."

Rose didn't want to be selfish but she so seldom got to beat Doris to some juicy piece of gossip. Especially something as juicy as this.

"If I don't tell her, she'll keep looking for who he is. If I do tell her, she'll keep looking for who he is, but she'll know enough to find him."

The curtains had stopped moving, the breeze had disappeared as it warmed from the sun. Rose took the silence as a sign. She just wasn't sure what it meant.

"Mercedes is in trouble either way. So what do I do?"

Rose thought about it for a moment, staring blankly at the window, waiting for a response.

"I find Mercedes. And once I find her, I watch her carefully. What does *she* want?"

She turned away from the window, thanking Mercedes—and Doris—for giving her something to concentrate on other than her son. She wasn't sure she'd have made it through the day without a distraction.

And not just any distraction would have done. She needed a major distraction, one that would engage her compassion.

Figuring out who had caused Mercedes's extremely peculiar behavior over the summer was probably the only thing that would work. Rose couldn't imagine anything else—except maybe Rowena Dale really getting married and not just engaged—that might involve her in this way.

Doing it without alerting Doris added another layer to her distraction and Rose needed all the layers she could get.

Because underneath her window-gazing, her contemplation of Mercedes and her morning man, lay the knowledge that it would only be a few hours before she'd know the truth. Even if she didn't want to know it, Doris would tell her.

Doris, like Sam and Mercedes, always knew what was right for Rose. She had spent her grown-up life counting on them to show her the path.

And while she counted on them, while she allowed herself the luxury of not having to decide what was right, what needed to be done, Rose could concentrate on her special gift. And even that she had learned about from them.

It wasn't something she'd ever thought about, though once they'd pointed it out to her, she realized she'd been doing it her whole life.

Rose's ability to see manifested itself quite differently than it did in Mercedes or Doris. Her ability was linked to only one emotion—despair. She sympathized with everyone, she listened and soothed, but her real ability was to see despair.

Despair so often hidden itself in grief or pain or anger, even more often in resignation, an inwardness that couldn't connect to others, to possible relief, but Rose saw right through all of those emotions and zeroed in on the despair. That's how she knew to send people home with the sergeant, that's how she knew that they needed more than just sympathy.

She would sit next to them, almost touching, and say nothing. Because despair was so all-emcompassing conversation was impossible, sympathy was disregarded, even the best advice went unheard.

But her skill, as important and unusual as it seemed, was seldom needed.

Rose had never really considered this before, but both she and Mercedes had skills that were seldom required, while Doris, her practicality and straightforward get-to-it-and-solve-the-problem attitude, were needed on a daily basis.

Rage fuelled Mercedes's goddess of justice persona. It wasn't the rage of others, though, it was the rage Mercedes felt for someone else's pain. Mercedes didn't feel that anger very often. When she did, everyone around her backed away while the goddess did her job.

People didn't much like Mercedes when she was wearing her goddess of justice mask. Rose thought it scared them. Mercedes became a different person, a goddess, and goddesses were scary people. You never knew what they would do.

Rose, though, Rose just stayed herself. A little more insightful, maybe, but no different than she was every single day of her life. *What happens*, she thought, *is that my entire being concentrates itself on another person and I feel what they feel.*

Maybe that was because of the baby. Rose had spent all of his life trying to ward off the despair she felt about him. She knew it intimately.

Doris was a whole other matter. Because she didn't show her emotions—or at least she hadn't until this extraordinarily odd summer—Rose couldn't tell how Doris felt about the things she did and the people she helped.

Doris just looked at a problem and she solved it. Rose loved that about her.

Well, now it was Rose's turn to do something. Even if she didn't know exactly what it was, she did know that it began with finding Mercedes.

"That was easy," she said to Mercedes, who had somehow snuck up the path without Rose hearing her footsteps on the gravel.

"What?"

"I decided I needed to find you and there you were."

"What are you doing here? You should be at work." Mercedes looked at her watch. "You should *definitely* be at work. Sam must be frantic."

"You're right. He's probably frantic. It's good for him, makes him see how much he needs me." Rose smiled at Mercedes and they spoke in unison, "Not that he'd ever forget that."

"Sam is the best husband I know," Mercedes said, a little wistfully, Rose thought.

"Yeah, well, he's one of the only husbands you know."

"Isn't that odd?" Mercedes appeared to contemplate Rose's statement. "Me. Doris. Rowena. Julie."

"You can't include Julie, she's getting married in a month."

"She's not married yet and I can include her if I want. Almost everyone one we know is single or divorced or widowed. This town is an actuarial paradise."

Rose laughed and changed the subject. She didn't care about Sam or actuaries. She wanted to know where Mercedes had been that morning.

"Where have you been?"

"Walking on the beach."

"You've been doing that almost all summer, haven't

you? That's why I never see you at the Way-Inn for breakfast."

"By the time I get back from my walk, I'm into check-outs and cleaning. But it's almost Labor Day and I can't wait."

Rose waited and said nothing. Sometimes it worked with Mercedes and sometimes it didn't. This time it worked.

"It's been a rough summer," Mercedes said. "The wedding and Doris and Tonika and Emily."

"And me," Rose said quietly. "You've had a lot to deal with and you've spent most of the summer helping the rest of us out. You've been a rock."

Mercedes leaned against the bedroom window and stared out at the trees.

"I haven't felt like a rock. Not a bit. But compared to you and Doris? I've had an easy summer."

Rose wasn't so sure of that. There was something going on under Mercedes's refusal to take her own problems seriously. She'd had no trouble admitting to her envy of Julie, but that seemed to have faded. Mr. X—whoever he was, and Rose couldn't stop herself from speculating—was a problem.

She couldn't help herself. "Is he married?"

Mercedes looked off into the trees for a few

moments before she answered. And when she did, it didn't help.

"I'm not talking about it," she said, her voice gentle but sure. "Not now. And I don't want you and Doris to talk about it either."

"We won't," Rose insisted. "We promised."

"So why are you asking me about it?" Mercedes asked, hands on her hips and the goddess of justice mask faintly visible through her regular face.

"Because I can't help myself," Rose said. "Because I'm trying to get through the next few hours without falling apart. You're a distraction. Mr. X is a distraction."

"Oh, honey, what's happened?"

Rose didn't want to change the subject. She wanted to know about Mr. X and she wanted to know *now*.

"Nothing has happened. I want to know about Mr. X. I won't even tell Doris if you don't want me to."

She could see Mercedes hesitating, could almost see the wheels spinning inside her head.

Is Rose really going to fall apart? What should I do? Do I tell her? Will that really help?

But before she had been able to imagine the next sentence, Rose knew what the final result would be. Mercedes would insist on knowing what was happening with Rose. She wouldn't insist as a way to avoid talking about Mr. X, although that would be the result. She would insist because she wanted to help Rose.

Rose acquiesced without another word from Mercedes.

"Doris is going to search the obits for me today."

"How is that going to help? It'll take months before she's even finished British Columbia and even if he's not there, it won't prove anything."

"I know when it happened."

"You know when what happened?"

It wasn't often that Rose was able to confound Mercedes. She didn't take any pride in it this time.

"I know when he must have... Well, you know."

Mercedes hugged Rose to her. "I know what you mean, but how do you know when?"

"Because I started doubting. And I know the week it happened. Doris only has to search for that one week."

"Oh," Mercedes said. "I see. And she's going to do that this afternoon."

"Yes. She promised she'd call me as soon as she found anything."

Rose shivered in Mercedes's arms.

"Will you spend the afternoon with me?"

"Of course I will. But—" she gave Rose a little shove "—you'd better get back to work. And I'd better get my butt in gear. I'm already—" she looked at her watch "—an hour behind."

Rose wiped the tears from her face, and then did the same to Mercedes.

"I can do it," she said. "I just need to know."

CHAPTER 24

I felt bad about feeling happy that Rose needed me this afternoon. But it didn't stop me from feeling a kind of guilty joy about it. Because if I'd thought that the summer days were dragging before this morning, today was worse than I could have imagined. I could already feel the hours before tomorrow's dawn dragging in front of me like a trek across the Sahara.

If it weren't for Rose, I wasn't sure I'd make it. Her news had given impetus to my day, wings to my feet.

Because I had to get to the Way-Inn before Doris left the gossip queens' booth. I had to talk to her before she set off on her errand for Rose.

And then I would spend the afternoon metaphorically holding Rose's hand. And maybe literally as well. I knew I'd spend at least part of the afternoon picking up broken cups and plates and glasses. Another part of it would probably be spent following around behind her to make sure that coffee cups were refilled and orders were taken correctly.

Rose had been having trouble with breakage and order-taking all summer. Today was sure to be the worst of all.

Waiting was hell.

I raced through the rooms, glad that no one was checking out. It meant tidying up and changing sheets and towels rather than a full-blown disinfecting and cleaning.

The vacuum zoomed through the rooms, the mop swifter than an eagle, the bathrooms gleamed in moments.

I stood in the parking lot and cursed the newlywed couple who sported a homemade Do Not Disturb sign on the door. You didn't get to wait until the afternoon to have your room cleaned at the Sand Dollar Motel. It happened before eleven or it didn't happen at all. If they didn't get up and out of that bed in five minutes, they'd have to clean their own room.

They didn't.

I left them towels and clean bedding on the chair outside the door and tamped down the envy that swept through me.

"Mercedes Jones, you are just going to have to get over this."

Waiting was hell.

The Way-Inn buzzed when I arrived shortly after eleven, showered and dressed in the brightest thing from my closet. Fuschia shorts, sunshine-yellow shirt and matching sneakers.

Rowena Dale blinked and pulled her sunglasses from her purse when she saw me coming in the door. I grinned and waved. It wasn't easy to shock Rowena. I put another tick against my day.

Two kisses from Joseph. Tick.

Rose's distraction. Tick.

Shocking Rowena. Tick.

Things weren't going anywhere near as badly as I had expected they might. Now if only I could convince Doris. I poured myself a cup of coffee and yelled, "Hash browns for me, Sam," as I passed the kitchen.

I slid into the already-warm seat opposite Doris. "Been busy, have you?" I asked.

"It has been very busy this morning. Are you here in an official capacity?"

I laughed. Doris cracked me up when she got on her high horse. What she really wanted to say, and was unable to, was that I was intruding into her space. We had appointed her to be the summer gossip queen and she wanted it all to herself.

"Of course not," I soothed. "You're the summer queen. I need some help."

Doris's eyebrows met over her nose.

"If you keep doing that, your perfect forehead is going to get wrinkled. You've spent almost seventy years with your serenity showing on your face. Don't stop now."

"I am not sure I can help myself."

Her forehead wrinkled again.

"Isn't easy, is it? Once you've let one of those emotions out, the rest just follow right on behind. Not to worry, hon. You could live another thirty years and still look like you were half your age. Even if you do spend all that time showing your emotions on your face."

"I thank you for that," Doris said, smiling a smile so wide it might almost have been called a grin.

I was so used to guessing at Doris's emotions that seeing them show up right clear on her face like that was a distraction.

Seeing Doris's emotions on her face. Tick.

This was turning into a very much better day than I had expected.

"I need to talk to you about Rose."

"Ah," she said. "I understand. I tried to call you this morning."

The question she wouldn't ask shone on her face and I congratulated her on her restraint.

"I'm proud of you, Doris. You didn't ask. But I'll tell you anyway. I was walking on the beach and when I got home, Rose was there. She told me about your search."

"I wanted to speak to you about that this morning. I wanted to ask you to spend the afternoon here."

"Julie brought her to-do list over with her. She'll keep an eye on things at the Sand Dollar."

I tried not to think about the afternoon siesta I thought she and Ron might take in my living room.

"You are still having trouble with Julie and Ron, yes?"

"Yes. But it's not as bad as before."

"Of course not. You have a man of your own to worry about. Did you see him this morning?"

Doris didn't even look sheepish as she asked the question.

"I'm not talking about it."

I wanted to say 'I'm pleading the Fifth,' or 'I'm calling my lawyer,' but 'I'm not talking about it' was as close as I could get. Doris watched the same cop shows I did and she wouldn't hesitate to tell me that I wasn't in a jail cell or being questioned by a police officer.

"Just a friendly question," she'd say, her glee at beating me clear on her face.

I repeated it. "I'm not talking about it. Not yet."

"All right, Mercedes. We can talk about it later."

I watched as she made a note in her purple notebook. Doris always had two notebooks with her at the gossip queens' booth. The purple one was for reminders, gossip to be followed up, stories to be sniffed out. The red one was for things to do.

I was now an official story. Oh, surprise.

"Doris? Can we get back to Rose?"

Doris nodded graciously—she had the bearing of a queen—and took a practiced sip of her jasmine tea.

"Although you do not have to tell me what you want. You want me to delay the search. You want me to lie to Rose. You want me to..."

"I want you to allow Rose to retain her faith in her boy. I don't want you to find any boys of his age dead in that week. I want you to lie to Rose."

"I can do that," Doris said, "but are you sure it is the right thing?"

I thought about it for a few moments. I wasn't sure. How could anyone be sure about a thing like this? But I was worried. What if the knowledge was too much for Rose.

"I don't know. Do you?"

Doris shook her head. "No. But I think that it may be the best thing. To delay the knowledge until the summer is over. It will be too much in August."

I wasn't sure there'd ever be a good time to tell Rose that her son was dead. But September would be better than August so I nodded in agreement.

Rose's voice rose above the clatter of the kitchen and the hum of the customers.

"Hello," she said. "You're back."

She was talking to the young man I'd wondered about at the beginning of the summer. He looked better than he had the last time I'd seen him, healthier, stronger. I hadn't thought of it when I'd first seen him, but he had looked then as if he were recuperating from an illness or an accident.

Now he looked as if he'd spent the summer surfing or running on the beach. Even more, I was certain that he was someone I should know.

Once again, I went through the list in my mind. Waiter. Ferry employee. Tourist. Delivery man. And I knew he was none of them.

"Doris?" I asked the queen of television. "Do you recognize that boy?" I pointed across the room to the table by the window, the same table he'd sat at the last time he'd been in the Way-Inn. "The one Rose is talking to."

Doris peered across the café, her eyes squinting.

"You're doing it again. I think you need new glasses."

"That is none of your business. The sun is at his back. I cannot see him very clearly. Why do you ask me this question?"

"Because he looks familiar. Maybe he's an actor?"

Her face lit up. Doris loved actors and singers and dancers and painters. She loved celebrity, even the minor types of celebrities we occasionally celebrated on the Sunshine Coast. She had sat in the front row of the writers' festival ever since its inception and could tell you stories about each writer who had appeared before her.

But an actor? In the Way-Inn? Doris rose from the booth, her grace wavering under the excitement. I watched as she banged her hip on the table edge. The grin on my face widened when she hit Rowena Dale's arm and sent her tuna salad sandwich flying. But even Rowena couldn't stop Doris in full running.

She stopped next to Rose and I could see her nose quivering. Doris would sniff out who he was. I hoped she wouldn't do it too soon. I was enjoying the view. Doris's excitement and Rose's smile made me happy.

Made me forget about my own problems and urge them on. "Come on," I whispered to Doris. "Don't give up. Ask him. Use your interrogation skills on him rather than me."

She must have heard me because she sat down across from him and started talking. I didn't need to hear her voice to imagine the conversation. I had sat in on hundreds like it.

Career?

Education?

Marital status?

What are you doing on the Sunshine Coast?

The oddest thing about these interrogatories was that the person being interrogated didn't seem to mind at all. Even more surprising, most people seemed to like it, as if grateful that someone, finally, took an interest in their life.

Within five minutes, Doris and the young man were chatting like old friends. Rose had stayed, leaning against the third chair back, her head turning from the boy to Doris and back again.

I was fascinated by the picture the three of them made. It felt as if there was something between them, something more than a chance-met acquaintance, something more than just a cup of coffee and a muffin.

And it bugged me that I couldn't figure it out, especially because it was so obvious. They leaned in toward each other like Doris and Rose and I did when we were telling each other secrets. They laughed like they'd known each other for years. Even Doris laughed.

I wasn't the only person who noticed, either. Rowena Dale's sunglasses were turned toward that table and I wasn't surprised when she got up from her table and wandered over to sit down in the booth opposite me.

"Who's that boy?" she barked.

"I don't know. I've seen him here before. Once. But he's sure a hit with Rose and Doris."

"Humph. There's something odd about that, something I don't like. He looks familiar."

I waited for Rowena's take on the boy. It was sure to be entertaining. She didn't really like men all that much although she was always tempted by them. I couldn't blame her for the dislike. She'd had terrible luck with men, but this boy? He seemed more than okay to me. And I trusted Rose and Doris. They were the least likely women in the world to be fooled by a crook or a creep.

"I bet he's a grifter. I've seen his like before. Fresh-faced pretty boys, all of them."

I looked over at the table by the door. The three of them had settled in for a good long talk. I recognized the symptoms. There was a story behind Rowena's statements and now I was sure that Rose and Doris were okay, I wanted to hear it.

"How do you know that?"

I'd learned over the years that I couldn't ask Rowena straight out about a man in her past. I needed to sneak up on it.

"How do you know he's a grifter?"

She looked at me, suspicion in her eyes, but Rowena could never resist telling stories, especially the ones that put men in a bad light. She spent most of her time making sure that everyone knew that her status as a spinster wasn't her fault; it was the fault of all the terrible men out there.

"It was a long time ago. I met him in Las Vegas, before it became a circus. When gambling was gambling and real men played poker, not these lightweights you see every single night on television."

Rowena would have spat if she wasn't in the Way-Inn. Rose had trained her out of that bad habit years ago. It didn't stop Rowena from spitting everywhere else, but as Rose often said, it was a start.

"We were in the casino at the Sands. Dean and

Frank and Sammy were playing that week and I thought maybe I'd get to meet one of them. Instead I met Joey. Big-time gambler, big-time grifter.

"He charmed me out of—well, more money than he should have. But it wasn't about the money. It was about the charm. I really believed he wanted to marry me. He really made me believe that he'd love me forever. Yeah, for all of five minutes.

"I had to call my banker to send me enough money to get back home. And Joey looked exactly like that boy over there. Exactly."

I knew what bothered Rowena the most was having to call her banker. She never liked anyone to know she'd made a fool of herself, especially someone she had to ask for favors.

I looked over at the boy one more time. I just couldn't see it.

"Rowena? He looks nice to me. And Rose and Doris like him. It's not often those two get fooled."

"Well, I'd be willing to bet my fortune that they're getting fooled right this very minute."

She picked up her bag, settled her sunglasses more securely on her nose, and flounced off, leaving me to pay for her tuna salad sandwich.

Doris and Rose were okay. I was sure of it. Or at least

I was sort of sure of it, but obviously not quite sure enough of it to leave it alone.

"Sam?"

I had waited until he'd put down the cleaver before I came up behind him. Sam wasn't normally a jumpy man, but living with Rose during the past summer might have made him so. I took precautions just in case.

"Good time for a break," he said, looking around his spotless kitchen with a grin of satisfaction. "You want a coffee?"

"I always want a coffee. But first I want you to take a look at something. Do you know that boy Rose and Doris are talking to? Rowena thinks he's a grifter. He was here at the beginning of the summer, too."

Sam ambled over to the pass-through. I waited for him to turn and say, "Nope, never seen him before," but he stood as still as a coyote waiting on a cat.

"Sam? Something wrong?"

"You mean you haven't seen it? Of course you haven't. No one has."

"No one's seen what? Should I call Ron?"

Sam still hadn't moved. His body trembled and he carefully placed a hand on the counter, as if to hold himself up. I'd never seen Sam like this.

"Sam? Should I call a doctor? Come on, Sam, you're scaring me."

His whisper was so low I could barely hear it over the voice of Van Morrison on the radio.

"That boy is Rose's son."

CHAPTER 25

If Sam hadn't rushed from the kitchen to catch her at the exact moment he did, Rose would have ended up face-first on the floor. And embarrassed herself right in front of her son.

Whose name she still didn't know. She thought he might have said it just before she fainted, and that was embarrassing enough, but if he had, she'd missed it.

Doris will know, she thought. *She'll remember. If the whole thing wasn't just a dream.* Which was the reason Rose wasn't opening her eyes. If it was a dream, she didn't want to wake up. Not just yet.

"Rose? Rose?" Doris called her name from a long way away. "Rose? Wake up. It is time to wake up."

Rose didn't respond. She couldn't.

"Rose, babe?"

She didn't respond to Sam, either.

"Rose? Get your damn eyes open right now. Or else."

Rose still didn't open her eyes. Not until a glass full of cold water—one containing a few sharp-edged ice cubes—hit her face. Rose could always count on Mercedes to do what needed to be done, even if she didn't like it.

She opened her eyes.

Rose lay on the floor of the Way-Inn looking up at four faces peering down at her. The faces were distorted and it took her a while to identify them.

Mercedes, as calm as always, with an empty glass in her hand. Doris, her face shaped by an odd combination of joy and fear. Sam's face right next to hers with his arm around her back, lifting her from the floor.

"This floor is filthy," was the first thing Rose could think of to say. "Get me off of it."

Mercedes laughed, a glorious laugh, completely at odds with the statement.

And Rose finally turned to look at the fourth face. Her boy. She hovered between belief in his presence and sheer panic at the depths of her insanity. Doris saved her.

"Rose, this is Patrick Joseph King. Pat, your birth mother, Rose."

Rose sat wrapped in Sam's arms—it was the only way she could support herself—and looked across the table at Patrick.

"Call me Pat," he said. "I've been Pat since I was five years old."

Rose tucked away that snippet of information. Pat. Her boy was called Pat.

"I don't know why I didn't figure it out weeks ago," Mercedes said. "The first time I saw you—" she smiled at Pat "—I thought you looked familiar. You do. You look just like Rose."

He grinned back at her, a lock of hair falling over his forehead.

"Yeah, I do, don't I?"

"Rose. Pat. Why not move back to our booth? It will be more private." Doris waved her arm around at the dozen or so regulars watching with avid eyes.

Sam helped Rose to her feet.and over to the booth, followed by Pat. Doris and Mercedes circulated through the Way-Inn, picking up checks and murmuring, "This one's on us," while hurrying the customers out the door.

Once the last person was gone, Mercedes went over to the booth.

"We're out of here," she said. "The customers are gone and Doris is just putting up a sign to say you'll be open again in the morning."

Sam nodded and heaved himself out of the booth.

"I'll walk you to the door and lock it behind you." He glanced over at Rose and Pat, engrossed in each other. "I'll pull the blinds."

Sam had to raise his voice to be heard by the two still in the booth. "I'll make dinner, okay? It'll be ready at five. Doris? Mercedes? Why don't you come back for dinner?"

Doris and Mercedes nodded. Rose knew they'd say nothing about Pat's arrival, not before then. Doris wouldn't say anything, even to Gray and Josie. And Mercedes? She'd go back to the Sand Dollar and she'd wait for dinner.

"Can you stay, Pat?" Sam asked.

"Of course. I need to catch the late ferry but it's not until nine."

Rose dared not take her eyes from Pat's face. She found herself repeating his name under her breath. She watched him and wondered if her unrelenting stare made him uncomfortable.

It didn't seem to. He sprawled in the booth like any young man, his hands relaxed on the table, his face cheerful, as if meeting his birth mother was the most natural thing in the world. And maybe it was.

"I always knew I was adopted, it's one of the first things I can remember knowing about myself. And when I got sick in the spring, Mom told me it was time to look you up."

"I knew it," Rose said. "I knew something was wrong."

"I got some virus—they never did figure out exactly what—while I was in Mexico over spring break. I was in the hospital for weeks, sick as a dog. Mom told me afterwards that they weren't sure I would make it.

"So here I am."

"I'm glad," Rose said, her words completely at odds with her real feelings. She wasn't sure she could express them in words, so settled for watching her son's face.

"Your parents are okay with this?"

"It was Mom's idea."

Pat said that with an air of complete certainty. If his mom said it, it would be done.

Rose waited for the envy to kick in because it was so obvious how much Pat worshipped his mother. But it didn't. She took a few extra moments to make sure. Nope, still no envy. No pain, either.

The black hole she'd been ignoring, that aching sense of loss she'd been carrying for almost twenty-five years was gone, vanished as if it had never been.

She smiled at Pat and said, "Tell me about yourself."

CHAPTER 26

The Sand Dollar was too small to hold my happiness. First Doris, then Rose, had found their heart's desire and I could see the joy in their faces. But even more than joy, I saw peace and I envied them.

I didn't want to look in a mirror, not now. Because I wanted, desperately, what I saw in their faces. I had ruined my summer with envy—turned my life green with it—and now I wanted it to be over. I wanted my story to be resolved.

My lust and longing were so trivial compared to the pain Doris and Rose had suffered over the summer. I *didn't* have a child in pain; I *didn't* have a missing child.

What I had was something that should have brought me joy rather than envy. I had a beautiful daughter, a daughter who was the most beautiful woman in the world, and she had found the man of her dreams. And they were getting married.

And all I could think about was myself.

"Mercedes Jones," I said to the mirror where I was examining my face for traces of green. "Get over yourself. Whatever is bugging you is nothing. Not compared to Doris or Rose. Not compared to Rowena Dale. Not compared to almost everyone you know."

I leaned in closer to the mirror and pulled down the skin under my eyes. Maybe the green was under my eyelids. Because I was absolutely, one-hundred-percent, securely and completely certain that it was somewhere on my face.

No one could feel the envy I'd been living with for months and not show it somehow. It was there. I just couldn't find it.

I stripped the bright-pink T-shirt off over my head and headed for the full-length mirror in the bedroom. On the way, I turned on all the lights. The overhead light. The two bedside lamps. The floor lamp in the corner by my reading chair.

I opened the door to the closet and turned on the light in there. And then I opened the blinds, anchoring them at the top of their reach.

The pine trees out the window shimmered in the sun and I opened the window and took a deep breath filled with salt and pine and the sweet scent of wildflowers. Those smells weren't what I wanted. I wanted the beach. I wanted Joseph.

But I returned to contemplation. Because I didn't want to go to him with envy coloring my body.

I turned the mirror to face the window so the light came in over my shoulder, so I could get the best possible view of my body as I examined it.

My shoulders were fine, freckled and tanned from the summer sun. I pulled off my bra and checked my breasts, nipples first. They were their usual warm pink, and my breasts were as white as the rest of my untanned skin, only the fine blue veins marring their paleness.

I turned away and looked over my shoulder. My back showed no signs of green, nor my arms.

I stepped out of my shorts and my panties. No green, not anywhere. Not on my legs or my knees or my ankles or my butt. Not even the faintest hint of it.

But as I searched, my body changed color. I could see it change in the mirror. Starting with my face, and without my consent or knowledge, my entire body blushed like the palest of pink roses at the beginning of summer. The pink even reached my toes, turning my tanned feet pink.

"Now what?" I complained to the mirror. "What does this mean?"

A low growl spoke from the window behind me.

"It means, Mercedes Jones, that what was always going to happen between us is going to happen a whole lot sooner than I planned."

Joseph stepped through the window as if it were a door, his long legs making light of the height of it. He carried a handful of dahlias, the blooms as large around as both his beautiful hands. Purple so dark it was almost black. A yellow so clear and bright it hurt to look at. Orange like the sun setting on a late-fall afternoon.

He handed them to me and stood back.

"People on the Sunshine Coast call your daughter the most beautiful woman in the world," he said, his head tilted to one side as he examined me. "They're wrong."

The dahlias dropped from my hands to the floor as he stepped toward me, ripping his shirt from his body as he moved. The rest of his clothes fell at my feet to join the dahlias.

A single step later, he was naked and I was in his arms.

We stood, for a moment, wrapped so tightly around each other I wasn't sure whether it was his heart or mine I felt beating so quickly, so passionately.

His breath stirred my hair, my lips touched the hollow at the base of his throat. His arms tightened around me and I knew he could feel me smile against his skin.

"Mercedes?"

I heard the question he didn't speak.

"Yes," I said. "Now."

I thought his body shivered against mine, but again I couldn't tell whether it was him or me. And again it didn't matter.

"It's been a long time," he whispered against my ear as he reached down to cup my face in his hands.

"Yes," I said, "I know," and mirrored his gesture, taking his face in my hands and lifting my lips to his.

First kiss. So sweet, so gentle, so quickly turning as dark and rich as the dahlias at our feet. With the first touch of his lips to mine, I lost the ability to think.

I tasted the salt of the ocean on his lips, smelled the dark aroma of French roast on his skin. His mouth opened to mine and I trembled at the rich wet surge as our tongues met.

My bed, so lonely and cold these past months—these past years—turned to summer with the coming together of our bodies.

I sensed the heat of the unshaded sun on the sand, the rhythm of waves after a storm, the solid weight of the sun-warmed rocks on the spit. The taste of French roast and passion. And always, the scent of the ocean at dawn.

I opened my eyes as he entered me, our bodies slick

with sweat. He said my name, his beautiful voice tense, and I felt myself clench around him.

"Joseph," I answered. "Now."

I was lost. And found.

And whatever green I might have been hiding beneath my skin was gone. I'd sensed it before, though I couldn't see it; now I sensed its absence.

Because lying next to Joseph, my body relaxed and ever so well-loved, envy was the furthest possible thing from my mind.

The sun had vanished from the window and the room had cooled, drying the sweat from our bodies.

Barely able to speak, I muttered, "Shower?"

"Hmm. But I'm not sure I can stand up. Maybe a bath instead?"

"Even better."

I hadn't known how handy the big tub I'd had put in last winter would be, hadn't considered it as a tub for two, but both of us fit as if we belonged there, Joseph's long arms and legs wrapped around me.

I knew we were going to have to talk, about his life, about mine, about the possibilities. We were going to have to speak of our future, but not yet. Not yet.

So I spoke of Tonika and Emily and Richard and how much I'd enjoyed holding Emily. I spoke of Doris and how, at sixty-eight, she'd unearthed the woman she wanted to be.

"It was as if she'd ripped off a mask she'd been wearing her whole life to reveal a new woman. I've known Doris for twenty years and this week I can't stop watching her. I wait for her to smile, I search out the tiny lines between her eyebrows, I want to see her laugh lines develop. She has always been an amazing woman, but now it's as if she's increased her amazingness exponentially. I can't resist her face, she's so much more beautiful than she ever was."

I felt Joseph's voice as much as I heard it, the boom of it resonating across my ribs and back, swirling through my veins.

"I like Doris Suzuki. But she's not as beautiful as you. I think, Mercedes Jones, that you have always lived your life in your face, and everything you've done, the woman you've been, is there for everyone to see. You don't wear a disguise."

Tears choked me. I wrapped my arms around his over my chest and squeezed, trying to convey my feelings without speaking.

"And Rose," I said finally, having once again found my voice, "was glowing when I left the Way-Inn this morning."

I screeched. "Damn. I have to get going. I'm

supposed to be at the Way-Inn for dinner in—" I couldn't see the red numbers on the clock radio on the counter "—soon, definitely soon."

Joseph laughed and pushed me up and out of the tub.

"What time do you have to be there?"

"Five o'clock," I said, "and it's after that now."

"You'll be a few minutes late, but I'm sure they'll forgive you."

"Rose might not even notice I'm not there. But Doris will and I'll never hear the end of it.

"I don't want to go, not now. But..."

I wanted to ask Joseph to come with me. I wasn't ready to let him out of my sight, not yet, but I wasn't ready to ask him to change his life for me. *Maybe not ever*, I thought, *maybe I won't ever be ready*.

"It's Rose's boy. Pat. She's just found him and he has to leave tonight and she wants to celebrate. Well, Sam wants to celebrate, which is really the same thing."

I pulled towels from the shelves and handed one to Joseph while running a comb through my hair.

Just do it, Mercedes Jones, just ask him.

Joseph Kennaday was old enough and wise enough to be able to say no to me if he didn't want to join us for dinner. I knew that. But what if he said no? How would I feel about that? How would I feel about it if he said yes?

"Joseph." I hesitated, picking at my nails. "Did you want to join us for dinner?" I hurried into an explanation, hoping that it would make him more comfortable. "The restaurant is closed. It'll be just us. You, me, Rose, Doris, Sam, Pat. Maybe Tonika and Emily and Richard. That's it."

Joseph's smile almost split his face.

"And maybe Josie and Gray. And Ron and Julie. Rowena Dale. Fred, Josie's dad, and Florence. Fred won't go anywhere without her now he's found her. I've never known Rose to throw a party that wasn't jam-packed with people."

I could see him considering. Spending the afternoon with me was one thing, going to the Way-Inn to dinner was throwing away his hermit status with a bang.

There would be no way to keep the secret—Doris and Rose would immediately realize that Joseph was Mr. X—if we showed up at the door of the Way-Inn together. They wouldn't even need to see my face. Joseph's presence would be more than enough.

Oh, Doris and Rose would be discreet. They wouldn't say, even if they were thinking it, "So the two of you have spent the afternoon having wild monkey sex?" although Rowena Dale might not be so careful.

Rose especially would be concerned about Joseph.

Though, after this afternoon, I knew that her concern was no longer necessary.

Something had changed for Joseph between this morning and this afternoon. I wasn't sure what it was, but the thing—the reason for his withdrawal from the world—had been dealt with. He had decided today that he was going to live.

I didn't know how I knew that but it was obvious. It was in the way he handed me the dahlias, the way he touched me, the way he purred when I touched him.

It was obvious in his laughter.

Joseph would never again need to go home in Ron's squad car. That was clear. And so was his response.

"I'd love to have dinner with *all* of you," he said, taking my hands and rubbing the nervousness away. "But I want to spend the rest of the night with you. Alone."

CHAPTER 27

The sun lit the windows of the Way-Inn like a beacon as Mercedes and Joseph hurried down the hill toward it, Mercedes hurrying to keep up with Joseph's much longer stride.

The walk had never seemed so momentous and Mercedes was becoming less and less certain that she'd be able to walk in the door when they arrived at it. She concentrated on the feel of Joseph's hand in hers.

"It'll be fine, you know," he said. "A little curiosity..."

"You don't know those women very well if you think a little curiosity is going to cover it. They're going to be frothing at the mouth when they see us together."

Mercedes giggled, picturing Doris frothing at the mouth.

"Can you blame them? I'm the hermit. You're the mother of the second most beautiful woman in the world."

"No. I can't blame them. But they know how I feel about you," she said. "That's going to make it harder."

"How *do* you feel about me?"

The hand holding hers tightened.

"The same way you feel about me," she said, squeezing back until she felt as if their hands might have been melded into one.

"That's a cop-out if I ever heard one," he said. "You go first. If Doris and Rose know how you feel about me, so should I. I need some protection when I go in that door." He shivered. "They scare me."

"Chicken." Mercedes grinned up at him. "Of all the things I imagined about you, cowardice wasn't one of them."

"Oh, I'm a coward, all right. How do you think I became a hermit?"

"Not cowardice, love. Self-preservation."

Mercedes stopped in the middle of the sidewalk and turned her body into his, holding him around the waist.

"You're no coward, Joseph Kennaday. And I know everything I need to know about you."

"I will tell you," he said. "One day soon, I'll tell you. But what I'll tell you now is that I have a job."

"You do? On the Sunshine Coast?"

"Freelance. I'm a journalist. I have a contract to write a weekly column."

"Of course you do. What about?"

"Anything. Anything at all I want to write about. People. Places. Politics. Chess. Music."

He smiled down at her. "I can hardly wait," he said. "I've missed writing."

The Way-Inn had somehow sneaked up on them and the door was right in front of their faces.

"We're going in, aren't we?" she asked, the hesitation clear in her voice.

"Not yet. Not until you tell me."

"Damn you, Joseph Kennaday. I'm not sure I can live with a man who has the memory of an elephant." Her voice shook. "I'm not sure I can live with a man at all. I never have, you know."

"I'm not just any man, Mercedes. I'm *your* man and you know it."

"Yes," she smiled. "I do know it. And I'm your woman."

Joseph didn't smile, but the expression on his face was better than any smile could be. He lowered his lips to hers for a quick, light kiss, both of them knowing that anything more and they'd be turning around and running back up to the hill to the Sand Dollar.

"It's time," he said.

Ignoring the Closed sign, Joseph grabbed the handle and flung open the door. The party had started without them.

And they'd both been right.

The Way-Inn was full of people. Rowena Dale, Josie and Gray, Fred and Florence down from Sechelt.

All of Doris's family, Tonika perched in a chair carefully placed behind a table so no one would knock her leg, Emily being passed from person to person without her feet ever once touching the floor.

Julie and Ron, rushing from the crowd at the back toward Mercedes and Joseph. Julie throwing her arms around her mother, tears shining in her beautiful face. Ron shaking hands with Joseph and whispering something in his ear that made Joseph blush right to the tips of his ears.

Pat and Sam, the two of them bearing platters of food and drink from the kitchen, looking as if they'd worked together for decades rather than for only a single hour.

Doris and Rose, their faces shining with curiosity, standing together at the counter. Mercedes watched as they looked first at her and Joseph, then at each other.

They nodded solemnly, as if they'd known it all along, as if the relationship between Mercedes and

Joseph had been part of a plan carefully crafted by the gossip queens.

Doris would have come up with the idea. "Mercedes needs a man," she'd have said. "We need to find her one."

Rose would have sat quietly in the booth and then, with a smirk, would have said, "What about Joseph?"

"The hermit?" Doris would question. "Of course. He's the one."

But without Mercedes the plan would remain unimplemented. And they couldn't tell her about it. She wondered how long they'd had this plan in the backs of their evil little minds. She wondered if they'd talked about it all summer. She wondered if they'd enlisted Rowena Dale.

And she knew that none of it mattered. Plan or no plan, gossip queens or not, despite living through the summer from hell, Mercedes and Doris and Rose had found everything that mattered to them, and all of it was right here in this room.